Parish Histories 1

Dailly: A South Ayrshire Parish

Dailly:
A South Ayrshire Parish

BEING ARTICLES ON THE HISTORY OF THE

PARISH

by
George Turnbull, D.D.

edited by
Rev John Torrance, B.D.
United Free Church, Dailly

1908

Glasgow
The Grimsay Press
2004

The Grimsay Press
an imprint of
Zeticula
57 St Vincent Crescent
Glasgow
G3 8NQ

http://www.thegrimsaypress.co.uk
admin@thegrimsaypress.co.uk

Transferred to digital printing in 2004

First published in Great Britain in 1908
by Stephen and Pollock, Ayr

ISBN 1 84530 008 4

To the Memory

OF THE

REV. GEORGE TURNBULL, D.D.

WHO DIED ON 5TH APRIL, 1908

FOR THIRTY-NINE YEARS MINISTER OF THE

PARISH OF DAILLY

CONTENTS.

ILLUSTRATIONS.

EDITOR'S PREFACE.

FROM 1880 onwards the late Rev. George Turnbull, D.D., minister of the Parish of Dailly, was in the habit of contributing articles on the history and antiquities of the Parish to a supplement which he published monthly in connection with the Church of Scotland magazine, "Life and Work." These were written in a popular style for his parishioners, by whom they were much appreciated. In this present volume an attempt is made to group these articles together under convenient subjects, in the belief that their substance deserves preservation in a more permanent form. Considerable omissions have been made : but otherwise it has not been judged expedient to alter the articles except in Chapter I., which is a compilation of two separate articles. If these articles had had the benefit of revision by the hand of the author himself, the value of this book would have been much enhanced. However, it is hoped that it may serve as a small tribute to the patient industry and spirit of research by which the author was enabled to give us these vivid glimpses of the past history of this ancient Parish.

Very cordial thanks are due to the family of the Rev. Dr. Turnbull for rendering such aid as made the publication of these articles possible.

U.F. MANSE, DAILLY
September, 1908.

INTRODUCTION.

OUR Parish is a very interesting one, not only on account of its great natural beauty, but on account of its antiquities, with many of which our readers may have but a slight acquaintance. It cannot but be a good thing that every man should regard his own Parish with intelligent interest and affection. Local ties, even when nothing more is implied in them than attachment to a locality, are not to be despised as silent moral influences. One would like if our young people, on leaving home and going out into the world, would carry with them such a pride in their native Parish as would make them feel that they must never disgrace it, but always be a credit to it. And such local attachments may do good in other ways, by forming or strengthening bonds of union, and leading to mutual sympathy and help. " Clannishness " among our fellow-parishioners abroad or in our large cities, from that point of view, is very praiseworthy. We hope that our modest efforts may deepen our interest in " our Parish," and so contribute something in these directions.

A SOUTH AYRSHIRE PARISH.

CHAPTER I.

PREHISTORIC DAYS.

THERE are to be seen in many parts of England and
Scotland mounds of earth or rounded hillocks of various
dimensions—sometimes on heights, sometimes on lower
ground—bearing a general resemblance to each other.
The hand of man may be traced upon them in earthworks,
of which there are usually more than one line, partially or
wholly surrounding them at different elevations. Some of
these lines are circular; others are more of an oval
shape. They were evidently thrown up for purposes of
defence. There are seldom any traces of stonework in
them, though there may have been wooden palisades to
give additional strength; and there may also have been
wooden habitations in the centre, but all traces of these
have now entirely disappeared.

These prehistoric forts are called by antiquarians
"motes." The root of the word is probably Anglo-Saxon,

and is a word meaning *dust*—hence "mote" in the sense
of "a speck of dust." In the French *motte* and Italian
motta the word develops into "a clod of earth" or "a
detached eminence, natural or artificial," and hence in
English the word has come to be applied to these ancient
mounds.

Motes constituted the fortresses of Saxon England for
some centuries before the Norman conquest. But they
were not peculiarly *Saxon*. In fact they are more
numerous in *Celtic* Galloway than in any other part of
Scotland. One of the most perfect and best preserved
specimens is in our neighbourhood. It is called Dinvin,
two-and-a-half miles E.S.E. of Girvan. It is in a
commanding situation. The summit is oval, 87 feet by 54
feet, and is surrounded by two well-defined ramparts with
intervening trenches.

One of the greatest authorities on this subject is Dr.
Christison, the secretary of the Society of Antiquaries of
Scotland.* Some three years ago, in the course of his
explorations, he visited our parish. I had much pleasure
in acting as his guide in an interesting antiquarian ramble.

KIRKHILL.

We first of all visited Kirkhill, where there is a distinctly
marked specimen of the ancient circular fort, and where
there is the additional attraction on a clear day of a
splendid view, embracing the firth and extending far into
the Argyllshire Highlands. Of this, Dr. Christison says:—
"Kirkhill, two miles N.N.W of Dailly, on the summit of

* Written in 1884.

the hill, 850 feet above the sea and 750 feet above the Girvan Water, nearly a mile-and-a-half to the south-east. A mound, one or two feet high and from 12 to 18 wide, encloses a nearly-circular space about 200 feet in diameter, within which, at the south side, there is a flat-topped mound, marked 'Tumulus' in the Ordnance Map, about 13 feet high and from 40 to 50 feet in diameter on the ill-

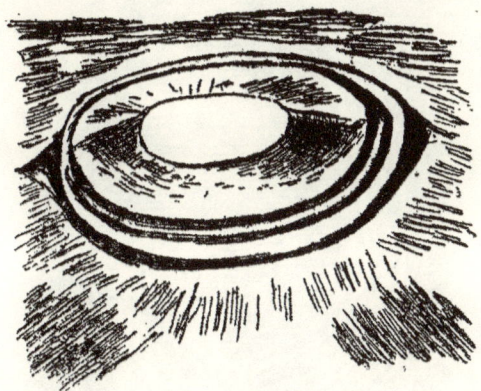

CAMP ON KIRKHILL.

From Smith's " Prehistoric Man in Ayrshire," by permission.

defined top, which is pitted with small squarish depressions. The ground is slightly trenched both outside and inside the enclosing mound. I have included this in the doubtful class, as it seems to be of an unusual type, and possibly is not a fort at all." Dr. Christison has suggested that the name *Kirk*-hill is a corruption of *Car ;* in Wales it occurs in the form of *Caer*, signifying a fort.

HADYARD (OR HADYET) HILL.

We then drove to Hollowshean farm, in Kirkoswald parish, where, on the small hill adjoining the farm, there is a triple line of circular earthworks on the side of the hill from which the position was most assailable. On the afternoon of the same day we walked to the top of Hadyet.

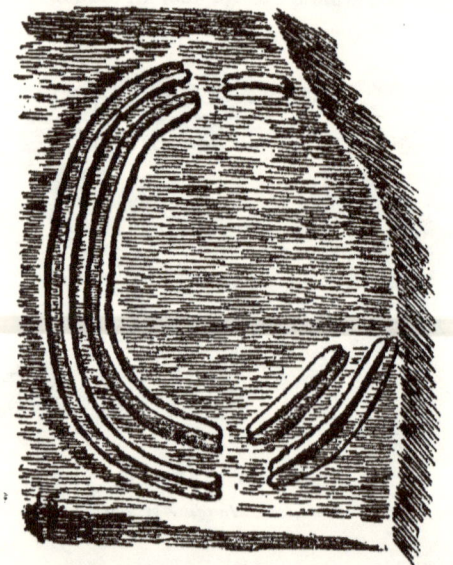

BRUCE'S CAMP, HADYARD HILL.
From Smith's " Prehistoric Man in Ayrshire," by permission.

According to tradition, which there is no reason to dispute, King Robert the Bruce had a camp there on the western extremity of the range. But we often find that in historic times advantage was naturally taken in military operations of ancient places of strength, and Bruce's camp on Hadyet, or the Trench hill, as it is sometimes called, appears to be an example. On returning, we walked part of the way along the ancient turf dyke, of unusually large dimensions, which extends right across the face of Hadyet, and ends at Craig, where it has had to give place to the plough, though no doubt in former times it continued its course much further. There is another dyke of similar dimensions extending inland in the neighbourhood of Stranraer, called the Deil's Dyke. Probably both were tribal boundaries.

Dr. Christison gives the following measurements :— "Hadyard Hill, one-and-a-half miles S.S.W. of Dailly, 1,028 feet above the sea, and 900 above Girvan Water, on the edge of a steep descent of 500 feet towards the stream north-westward. Here the work is open, but elsewhere a double mound encloses a central space of 270 by 230 feet. As they leave the edge the two mounds are close together, but they gradually diverge till they are 20 feet apart at the opposite end. To the south, perhaps from subsidence in the marshy slope, they have little relief, and are more like scarps on the hill-face. Elsewhere the mounds vary from 12 to 24 feet in width, and are never above four feet high to the outside. In the firmer ground to the north are some remains of a trench in front of them."

A PICTISH TURF VILLAGE?

Next day we went to explore certain mysterious earthworks on the farm of Blair. They are at the back of the farm, on what is called the Galloch Hill or Knockingalloch. The remains, though we must speak with caution, may indicate the site of an ancient British village. The habitations, if we may call them so, were huddled together, and were nine in number. The figure is more

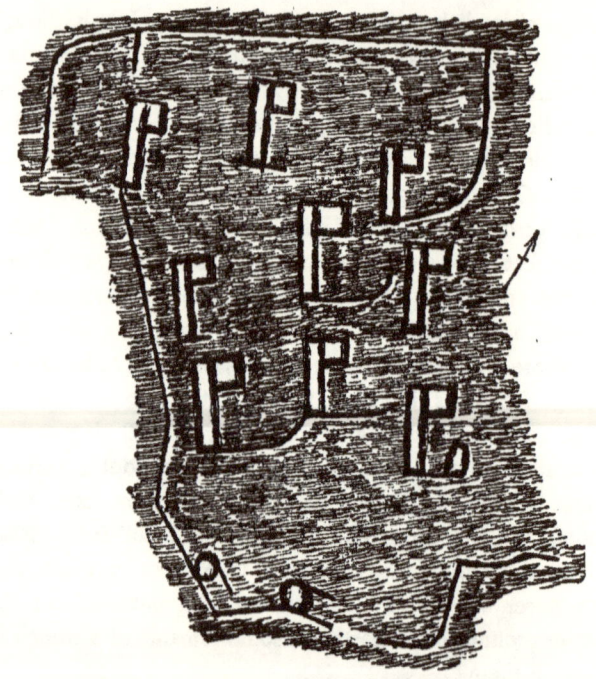

REMAINS OF TURF VILLAGE, KNOCKINGALLOCH.
From Smith's " Prehistoric Man in Ayrshire," by permission.

complete in some than in others. But the same formation can be traced in all, and they all appear to be of the same or very nearly of the same dimensions. The turf is on an average about 18 inches high and between two or three feet wide. Each figure has four sides, and is about 21 yards by about 10 or 11 yards. One of the four sides, always the one to the east, is convex, gently curving inwards, leaving, where it stops, an opening which seems to have been the entrance. On the opposite, or western side, there is an inner wall parallel to the outer wall, some three or four feet removed from it, but not extending the full length, so that a passage of some three feet is left at its extremity. At the other, or northern end of this inner wall, and turned towards the above entrance, is what appears to have been an inner apartment about seven yards square, one side of it being part of the northern wall, so that, roughly speaking, the inner wall and this enclosure take the shape of the letter P. Each " habitation " measures 21 yards by 11. The whole are surrounded by the remains of a protecting turf wall, including not only the so-called village but a considerable space not occupied by any dwellings. The entire space thus enclosed is about two acres, and measures from north to south 140 yards, and from east to west about 100. This enclosing wall is circular, except on the side where there are dwellings, of which it forms the outside boundary.

At three different points in this surrounding wall are the traces of what may have been watchtowers. There are no stones lying about, and if these were the dwellings of our primitive ancestors, they were probably completed with wood, which would soon disappear by fire or removal. Dr. Christison was greatly interested in the discovery. In the course of his antiquarian explorations he had never seen anything of the same description.

MOTE KNOWE, KILKERRAN.

Crossing the Newton Stewart Road beyond the " Deil's Elbow," we now made tracks through the hills for Dobbing-stone to see another interesting bit of antiquity marked on the Ordnance Survey Map, viz. :—the " Moat Knowe," —we have sometimes heard it called the " Cannon Knowe," situated at the point where the Kilkerran Burn and Delamford Burn meet and a short distance above where the Dobbingstone Burn joins the united, but at the time we saw it, very shrunken stream, which now flows under-neath the mouldering walls of old Kilkerran Castle. It was sometimes necessary to have places of strength for defence on the low ground as well as on the hills. Hence these " moats," circular mounds, either wholly artificial or raised upon natural knolls. They were surrounded by a palisade, and were encircled by a terrace or terraces, of which latter feature there are distinct traces in the Dobbingstone Moat. I observed, what had escaped my notice before, at the foot of the mound and exactly at the point where the two streams meet, distinct traces of a building.

Dr. Christison's description is as follows :—" The moat is oval, and stands out conspicuously by reason of its isolation, although closely overlooked from higher ground to the east and south. It appears to be partly natural, and stands from 15 to 25 feet in height, with steep sides except towards the east. The top measures about 90 by 30 feet. The base is surrounded by a strip of marshy ground, with remains of a rampart on the north and south sides On the south this rampart protects the trench-like marsh from the high ground outside. On the north there is a

descent to a terrace, which probably covered the whole
north face originally, but the western half has apparently
been carried away by the burn. At the foot of the west
end there are some signs of fortification or enclosure of the
small piece of the ground between the north and the
junction of the burns."

Following the dark hints which these silent records read
to us, we see our progenitors in this valley, clad in skins,
wild and unkempt, wandering through the woods with which
the valley was covered, armed with slings or bows and
arrows, or rudely cultivating a scanty crop in clearances in
the wood, yet never roaming far from their strongholds;
sometimes surprised and slain, their fort stormed, their
wives and families sharing their doom or carried off to be
slaves to the victors, who in their turn perhaps meet a
similar fate.

These green memorials, of which we have given such a
hasty sketch, gives us a vivid picture of the times wild and
rude, yet not without their uses in building up our nation's
manhood—times when there prevailed

> " The good old rule, the simple plan,
>   That they should take who have the power,
>   And they should keep who can."

CHAPTER II.

IN THE DAYS OF THE EARLY SAINTS.

ST. QUERANUS OR KIERAN.

TILL the 6th century after Christ, Scotland lay in heathen darkness and idolatry. But at that period light began to dawn. Columba, along with a devoted band of missionaries, sailed from Ireland and landed on the Island of Iona, called also after Columba, Icolmkill, but at that time named Hy. There he founded a monastery, which soon became a centre of light in the midst of the gloom. This was in the year A.D. 563.

Columba, we are told, had several "masters," who instructed him in the faith in early life. One of them was Kieran or Queranus, who has a special claim upon our interest. The ancient name of our parish, Dalmakerran, and still more clearly the name Kilkerran, indicate the presence and labours of the Saint among our savage progenitors. And this opinion is confirmed by the fact that there are undoubted traces of him, as we shall see, on the Cantyre peninsula, which is within sight of our Parish, and nothing would be more natural than for a man with the missionary spirit burning within him to hear and obey the cry of Macedonia wafted across the channel from our shores—"Come over and help us." We ought, therefore, to know as much as we can ascertain about one whom we might almost call, though his parish was far wider, "the first minister of the Parish of Dailly."

He seems to have been a great man in his day. Both throughout his native Ireland and Scotland his name was well-known and revered. Columba himself held him in high esteem, and is said to have written a poem in Latin praising him. A few lines have survived, of which the following may be taken as a translation:—

> " We praise Thee, O Christ, for the man,
>   So great an Apostle divine,
> Thou hast sent us our dark world to bless—
>   A lamp in this Island to shine."

Yet his origin was humble. He was called *Ciaran Macantsaor*, Kieran the son of the carpenter, and to this circumstance in common with the earthly life of his Master he is said to have added another, viz., he died at the same age, 33. But short as was his life, he seems to have used it well. He travelled far and near, like his brethren of the period, spreading the Gospel, and was not ashamed to turn his hand at times to other kinds of work. We get a glimpse of him in the Island of Aran "threshing corn for the community." We find traces of him in other parts of the country, but his name is most closely associated with Cantyre. He is called "The Apostle of Cantyre." We find there as well as here the name Kilkerran, a name which used to be given to the Parish of Campbeltown;

and the ruins of a church dedicated to him are to be seen in the centre of the principal burying-ground of the town and parish. There is a cave in the neighbourhood of the town which bears his name, and where he is said to have lived.

He died in the year A.D. 548, 15 years before Columba landed at Iona. The following is a prayer believed to be by him. The original, in Irish Gaelic, is preserved in a very ancient manuscript missal discovered in Drummond Castle in the end of last century:—"Alas, that a *learned clerk* (ecclesiastic or clergyman) should perish! O Thou Son (of God) have mercy on one devoted to Thy service. Heal and quicken my benumbed soul. Long have Thy visits been denied to my cell. Yet I should have quickly failed if Thou hadst not supported me. I will therefore, render Thee the tribute of my highest praise before the multitude of the people, and place whatever pangs I may endure to the score of my own sin and folly."

He is said to have composed a "lay" or short poem in which he prayed that God would give him long life for this end that he might devote it to His service, a prayer the spirit of which showed a closer resemblance to his Divine Master than is implied in the above coincidences. And although from his early death it appeared as if the prayer was not answered, yet we cannot doubt it was really answered in the sense of the Psalm—"He asked life of Thee, and Thou gavest it him, even length of days, for ever and ever."

Perhaps we may take the liberty of reviving this "lay."

LAY OF ST. QUERANUS.

A Lamp Columba called me, as they say,
   So be it, if it shine
Fed by Thine hand, O Lord, from day to day,
   With oil of Grace Divine.

*   *   *   *   *

Within my father's workshop as I stood
   Methought I heard the tread
Of Him whose brow with toil like mine was dewed
   In Nazareth's lowly shed.

Methought I heard his gentle accents plead:—
   "Comrade in earthly toil,
Thy partnership in nobler tasks I need,
   Upon Thy native soil

Plant thou my Cross, go tell men of their sin,
   And tell them of the Love
Of One who bled and died their souls to win—
   Tell of the Home above.

Nor only there, for other sheep I have,
   Now lost and wandering,
In yonder land of Albyn, o'er the wave,
   Them also thou must bring."

I hearkened, and I held the lamp He lit
   Amid Hibernian gloom ;
And, now to those who here in darkness sit,
   With light and life I come.

In this green valley, ramparted by hills,
   A winding river glides
Through wood and meadow, fed by murmuring rills,
   And seeks my native tides.

Within this dale, so fair, and yet so vile
   With dark idolatries,
Where crimson'd altars smoke to buy the smile
   Of demon deities.

Where through the glade the savage, rude and grim,
  Roams darkling to the grave ;
Alas ! they know not God—they know not Him
  Who poured His blood to save !

Here, in this leafy grove, I'll build my cell,
  O Christ, my Lord, to Thee,
And work and pray for souls Thou lovest so well,
  The dearer thus to me.

I fain would live, my Master, for Thy praise,
  But deaths around me fly ;
O spare me, Jesus—grant me length of days
  Thy name to glorify !—AMEN.

ST. MACHAR (MACARIUS.)

In addition to St. Kieran or Queranus there are traces
in our parish of another saint. On the farm of Whitehill,
where the ground begins to slope down to a small glen
called " Dalraichie Glen " (in Pont's map, published 1648,
" Glenryoch,") and a few hundred yards above Whirnie
Farm-house, is a spot named " Machrykill," or " Machar-a-
kill," the church or cell of Machar or Macarius. It used to
be sometimes called " the old graveyard." The spot was
enclosed and planted with trees a number of years ago by
the proprietor, the Right Hon. Sir James Fergusson, Bart.,
of Kilkerran. There are many people who remember having
seen what appears to have been the ruins of the chapel, or
a portion of the chapel, of the saint, in the shape of the
remains of four walls of very rude masonry, enclosing a
space of about 13 feet by nine feet. The stones have
now entirely disappeared, but a most interesting relic is still
standing in the form of a rude rectangular block of hard
freestone, four feet high, and slightly tapering from three
feet six inches by three feet two inches at the bottom to

two feet three inches by two feet nine inches at the top. There are two points about it which make it of exceptional interest.

First. The size.—In this respect, indeed, it may safely be said that this cross-pedestal is unique in Scotland. There are very few such pedestals, indeed, which are

PEDESTAL FOR CROSS, MACHRIKILL.

monolithic. The great bulk of them, especially those of later date, are *built* pedestals, having, it may be, a large flat stone on the top perforated to admit of the foot of the cross passing through it. This stone is sometimes nicely carved, as in one or two instances in Islay; or it may carry an inscription, as at Oransay: Generally it is quite plain, a mere top slab to keep the looser materials below from

B

being disintegrated. Sometimes there may be, indeed, as in the great cross at Oransay, a socket-stone imbedded in the lower part of this masonry, but independent monolithic pedestals are the exception, and not the rule. Even where they exist, their dimensions are comparatively small, the largest, that of St. Martin's Cross, Iona, hewn out of red granite, being not over half the height of this one at Machar-a-kill. It is only in Ireland where pedestals in any way approaching this one in size are to be found. There the monoliths—not plain as with us, but richly carved with all kinds of quaint and curious devices such as occur on our sculptured stones, groups of men and animals, illustrations of old times, and strange fancies — form familiar objects amid the rank growth and mouldering tombstones of her old churchyards. Even these, however, must yield both in size, and probably also antiquity, to this Scottish example. Gigantic as are the crosses of Tuam and Monasterboice, their pedestals do not equal it in dimensions, its nearest approximate being at Moone Abbey, illustrated by Henry O'Neill in his admirable work on the " Crosses of Ancient Ireland."

In mere point of size, then, this pedestal at Machar-a-kill is unequalled in Scotland, and rarely matched in Ireland. The direct inference is, that the cross it was designed to carry must also have been of noble proportions, standing upon the bare hillside, visible from afar over a wide range of country. The curious thing is, that while there cannot be the shadow of a doubt as to the purpose this pedestal served, not only have all vestiges of the cross itself disappeared, but all memory and tradition of it. Its loss and that of others on the same site may very possibly be due to the waves of destruction which swept over the country again and again during the Edwardian wars. So much, then, for dimensions, and the inferences to be drawn from them.

Secondly. The style of the pedestal.—It is true that we have not the very slightest decoration, the smallest trace of the sculptor's art to guide us on this point; but this pedestal is eloquent for all that in its own special way. When we remember that not only the pedestal, but still more the cross it was designed to bear aloft must have been a very important work in its time, we may well believe that the best skill of the period would be employed upon it. Had it been hewn then in any of the strictly architectural ages, say from 12th or 13th century downwards, we would have expected it to have shown a certain amount of technical or masonic skill. The stages would have been more or less regularly divided, and their lines of demarcation drawn sharp and true. Now the fact is, that with a distinct unity of purpose and idea, viz., that of hewing out a calvaried or triple-staged monolith, there is combined quite enough of irregularity in the execution to show that its sculptor was unacquainted with what we would call the use of square and level, and that he had his eye and inward purpose only to guide him. This fact gives a certain antique or primitive air to the relic, due no doubt to the fact of its very early origin. It comes before us as the work of one who wished to grasp and express the symbolic idea, without having at command those means of mechanical perfection we would expect so important a work to exhibit if erected during the period mentioned.

Fig. 2.—Although much smaller in its dimensions, this also is a very interesting and early pedestal for a cross. It is a rough block of freestone, with little or no hewing about it save what was necessary to excavate the rectangular socket which proves undoubtedly its former use. Besides this, there is on what we may call the face or front of the stone a smooth or polished space, on which has been carved a cross giving us a clue to the possible age of the stone

PEDESTAL FOR CROSS, MACHRIKILL.

itself, and therefore of the large upright cross it sustained. This small cross is formed by means of a broad line or groove marking off the outline, the centre of the arms being distinguished by a little pit or dot. The stone is broken away at the top, but the foot of the cross shows an important characteristic, the line bounding the rest of it (as will be seen from the drawing) being entirely omitted. Now this is in general limited to or most prevalent in very early work. It marks a transition stage, so to speak, in the mode of forming the symbol of the cross. There are two ways in which either this or any other figure may be expressed on stone, by incised lines or by cutting it out in relief. The way this little cross is fashioned partakes of both. The broad line running round it is certainly incised, but this is not the cross. It is the interior space the carver had in view as such, and has left out the line at the foot to show the cross as it were not inscribed on the stone but standing erect, and firmly planted in the ground. This is an extremely favourite mode of so representing the symbol in the earliest work we know of in Scotland. It occurs frequently on the tombstones in an old and long deserted Dalriadic burial ground on the shores of Loch Caolis-port, Knapdale, and also carved in the living rock in the Cave chapel at Cove in the same locality. This feature thus agrees with the early date we have assigned to the larger pedestal, strengthening the evidence as to the still earlier character of the site.

Mr. Cooper, then farmer at Whitehill, states that there was yet a third stone socketed in a similar manner, but that it has now unaccountably disappeared. This multiplicity of crosses on so small a site is certainly curious, but by no means unexampled. It may possibly mark the spot as a place of pilgrimage, such grouping of crosses, in what were considered sacred spots, being frequent both in Ireland and the Western Highlands, the peculiarity here being the smallness, or as we may say the insignificance of the site, the absence of all traces of interment, and the veil of complete oblivion time has gathered over it.

But who was this saint who has given his name to the spot? He comes down to us under a variety of names. Here are some of them :—Machar, Macharius, Mauritius,

Mocumna. There is a good deal in the history of him that is fabulous, as there is in the lives of many others of these ancient saints—such as the singing of angels around his cradle in infancy, his recalling a younger brother to life by lying beside his dead body, his healing lepers, and turning a wild boar into stone. Yet in the two last particulars the fabulous record sheds a lurid light on some of the physical aspects of our country in those early days. So far as we can gather the solid facts of his life, they were briefly these :—His father was an Irish chieftain. He was instructed by St. Columba in the Christian Faith, and taken with him to Iona, whence Columba sent him along with twelve companions into " Pictavia," where he was commanded to stay near a river bearing the form of a pastoral crook. There are traces of him as far north as Aberdeenshire, the church and parish of St. Machar, in Aberdeen city, being called after him. He is said to have built many churches, and to have been very successful in extinguishing the worship of false gods, and in turning many to the faith. Then St. Columba took him to Rome, where he was appointed Bishop of Tours in France, and there we lose sight of him. A metrical life of him by Barbour, who also wrote a well-known metrical life of Bruce, is said to be in the University Library, Cambridge.

The name, which has always been associated with the spot—we find it in the old map above referred to—coupled with the signs of a rude and very early age which the stone itself presents, leaves us little room to doubt that this old gray stone and the chapel with which it was connected date as far back as this St. Machar who came with St. Columba to Iona A.D. 563. We are thus fortunate in possessing in our parish one of the oldest and one of the most interesting relics of Christian antiquity to be found in Scotland.

MACHRYKILL.

"SERMONS IN STONES."

" Build me a temple to the living God
    Upon this green hill-side,
Whence I may sound His name and praise abroad,
    And tell of Him who died.

" No carven stones I crave, no sculptured saints,
    For souls are famished
For lack of knowledge, and my spirit faints
    To break the living bread."

Thus spake the saint, and straight the fane and stone
    The eager brethren raise;
And through the vale the Word of God was sown,
    With joy they hymned His praise.

And wild, rude men wept at the heavenly tale,
    Believed and were baptised;
Far flowed the healing stream o'er hill and dale,
    The wilderness rejoiced.

.   .   .   .

Gone saint and cell, yet still that stone, three planed,
    Beneath a three-fork'd tree
Adown our vale, by thirteen centuries stained,
    Proclaims the One-in-Three.

Gone saint and cell, ten thousand things are gone,
    Thou thy lone watch dost keep,
Like yonder sea-girt Ailsa, old grey stone,
    'Mid Time's devouring deep.

Thy treasures keep, O Time ! still dapple o'er
    Thy stone with lichen-stains;
But give us back the faith, from ages hoar,
    That made the mountains plains.

CHAPTER III.

KING ROBERT THE BRUCE.

THE ANCIENT BOUNDS OF THE PARISH.

OUR parish was originally much larger than it is at present. It included the greater part of what is now the Parish of Barr, and there is reason to believe that the district which is now the Parish of Girvan also formed part of it. The situation of our ancient church, about a mile from the western and south-western extremity of the parish, and six miles from its eastern boundary, and the fact that parish churches were generally central for the population, indicate pretty clearly that our parish originally extended much further in a westerly and south-westerly direction. Again, in the books of the Glasgow Commissary Court an entry is found, of date 1639, stating that Girvanmains is "in the parochin of Daillie." Girvan was a separate parish centuries before that date, but possibly the writer was either not aware of the change, or for some reason preferred to give the name of the original parish. At all events, we have a confirmation here of what on other grounds is extremely probable. Girvan seems to have been detached from Dailly towards the end of the 13th century. The

24

first indication we have of Girvan as a parish is in 1296, when "John, the Vicar of Garvan," swore fealty to Edward I. of England (Chalmers' Caledonia). Ailsa Craig should naturally have been included in the new parish, but, probably as it formed part of "the Barony of Knockgerran," it was allowed to remain in the Parish of Dailly.

In regard to Barr, "Kirkdamdie," the only chapel in the district having become ruinous, and also being inconveniently situated for the majority of the people worshipping there, a church was built in the village of Barr in 1652, a date cut in a stone in the eastern wall. That church was taken down when a new place of worship was erected. In the year following, viz., 1653, according to Barr Session Records, Barr was disjoined from Dailly and Girvan and constituted a parish.

But to return,—Seven hundred years ago the entire district was ruled, under the king, by one Duncan. He was created First Earl of Carrick in 1186. The Church of Dalmakeran, was in all probability built and endowed by him. At all events, it was handed over by him, with all its revenues, to the far-famed Monastery of Paisley, and the grant was confirmed by Alexander II. in 1236. Duncan afterwards, when he must have been advanced in life, gave a still stronger evidence of his attachment to the Church, if not of his piety, by founding, in 1244, the Monastery of Crossraguel. The Church of Dalmakeran, as was natural, was transferred from Paisley to the new monastery. This transference was effected by no less a personage than King Robert the Bruce, Fifth Earl of Carrick, whose name is connected with the district by other historical associations,

and the grant was confirmed to the Crossraguel monks by
Robert III. in a charter wherein the Church is called
" Ecclesia Sancti Michaelis de Dalmulkerane," from which
it appears that it was dedicated to St. Michael. Besides
other revenues, the monks of Crossraguel enjoyed the tithes
of five parishes, viz., Kirkoswald, Dailly, Girvan, Ballantrae,
and Straiton. In a return of the rental of the Abbey,
given in shortly after the Reformation, it was stated
that the Church of "Daylie" yielded 260 marks a year
(£14 8s. 10½d. sterling, amounting to about £140 of the
present value of money). The connection between
Dalmakeran or Dailly and Crossraguel continued till the
Reformation; year by year the tenants on the Church lands
sending across to the lordly abbot their tithes of corn, wool,
cattle, or salmon, he in his turn sending a chaplain to serve
the cure under his supervision. The abbot and his monks
were Benedictines of the Order of Cluny or Cluniacensians,
of which there were four houses in Scotland—at Iona,
Paisley, Fail, and Crossraguel. The founder of the Order
was Odo, Abbot of Cluny, or Clugni, in France, hence the
name. At first they were distinguished for their strictness
and spirituality, but at the period when they flourished in
our neighbourhood they seem to have degenerated. They
are said to have become addicted to ostentation and dis-
play in their places of worship. Hence they were
reproached by their rivals, the Cistercians, with having
churches " immensely high, immoderately long, superflu-
ously broad, sumptuously furnished, and curiously painted."
And such was the pride of the Order that at one time its
head laid claim to the title of " Abbot of Abbots," a

claim which was disallowed by a Council held at Rome in 1117.

KING ROBERT THE BRUCE.

Some of our readers may not be aware that among its other claims to honour our parish possesses that of having been at one time the residence of Royalty.

Our story begins in or about the year 1268. The scene is Turnberry. Travelling thither along the shore from Girvan one observes that the ancient raised sea beach, the foot of which the road has hitherto been following, has now receded some distance inland, leaving a broad tract of level land, a great portion of which is now sacred to early potatoes. Six hundred years ago this tract presented a very different appearance, being richly wooded and affording facilities for the chase, a favourite amusement of the lords and ladies of the day. Towering yonder over the trees, with the rude thatched cottages of dependents nestling around or scattered over the glade, is the lordly Castle of Turnberry, on the brink of a rocky precipice overhanging the sea, with its walls and turrets the grandeur and strength of which the present crumbling ruins, scarcely visible from the land side, but faintly indicate. On the site of the Castle now stands a lighthouse erected within recent years. Strange and suggestive meeting of the old world and the new—the old, hard, rugged, fighting, killing age, and the new, with its gentle, helpful, saving ministries. And the latter, built upon and rising out of the former, for the national life and character, such as they are, were then being "battered into shape and use." And if Scotland has anything of the character of a lighthouse, shedding its kindly, guiding light over the dark waters of the world, we know of one man who fought in and around these mouldering walls, who did much to lay the foundation.

At the time our story begins the owner of the Castle and its domains is a fair lady, the ward of the king, Alexander,—viz., Marjory, Countess of Carrick. She had been married, but while still young had been left a widow. Her husband was Adam de Kilconcath, or Kilconchar, Earl of Carrick. It was the time of the Crusades. Many of the Scottish nobles assumed the cross and set out with their following for Palestine. Among the rest was the Earl of Carrick, but, like so many others, he never lived to return. Two years after she had been left a widow, the Countess was engaged in a hunting excursion in the neighbourhood of the Castle, surrounded by a gay and gallant company of ladies and esquires in attendance, when a cavalier of noble and distinguished appearance cantered across her path. He was a Scottish knight of high birth, Robert de Bruce, son of Robert de Bruce, Lord of Annandale and Cleveland. He too had been a Crusader, and had gained renown in Palestine, but being a quiet, unambitious man, had returned to the peaceful enjoyment of his wealth and honours. The Countess saluted the knight, and courteously invited him to take part in the sport. Bruce, who was shrewd enough to see the danger of giving offence to the king by paying too much attention to his ward, declined, when the lady, giving a signal to her attendants to close around him, seized his bridle, and led him off by gentle violence to her Castle. Here, after fifteen days' residence, the romantic adventure ended in a marriage. The relations of neither party had been consulted, and, what was worse, the consent of the king had not been asked. Alexander was furious, and seized on the Countess' Castle and estate. Powerful friends, however, pled for the young couple, and he let them off with the payment of a heavy fine. And so Bruce in right of his wife became Lord of Carrick, and the first born of this romantic marriage was the great Robert Bruce, the hero of Scottish independence.

The disputes regarding the Scottish Crown, which began not long after this, at last ended in Bruce the younger being crowned by his few adherents at Scone, in the year 1306. The event was soon after followed by the disastrous battle of Methven, when Bruce's little army was surprised and cut to pieces before they could make any effective resistance. The king himself found refuge in Rathlin, on the north coast of Ireland. From thence, in the spring of 1307, he made another attempt to regain his Crown. Crossing over to Arran with three hundred followers, the king, misled by a false signal, landed on the Carrick coast, where he at once found it necessary to retire for a short way into the interior. He entrenched his small army, some three hundred strong, on the highest point of the Hadyet Hills, in our parish, commanding an excellent view of Turnberry Castle and the surrounding country. The remains of the entrenchment are still traceable on the summit, which is popularly known as the "Trench Hill."

Near the entrance to Knockgerran, and in a field on the opposite side of the road to Barr, there stands an upright stone which the Messrs. Mackie erected and inscribed with the name "Altichapel." According to tradition, a chapel of that name stood on the spot, and the general outlines of it can still be traced, though this is the only stone of the building that remains. Bruce, who was a very devout man, is said to have worshipped in this chapel while he was encamped on Hadyet. The spot is about a mile-and-a-half from the Trench Hill; and a short distance behind Knockgerran house is a spot where, across a small burn, there are a few stepping-stones, still designated "The King's Ford," and being in the direct line between the Trench Hill and Altichapel there seems no reason to doubt that it was so called because it was used by Bruce on his way to and from his devotions. We are told by Barbour in his metrical history of Bruce that he was in the habit of retiring daily for *privacy* to a small copsewood, between which and the camp a ridge intervened. Though no mention is made of a chapel, or of the object for which he sought privacy, it was probably for devotion, and the description applies to the site of Altichapel. There is certainly no copsewood there now, but we know that the hill country was in former times much more wooded than at present.

But whether it was here or elsewhere in the neighbourhood that he retired for privacy, on one of these occasions there occurred one of those narrow escapes and valiant feats of arms of which there are so many in his history. He was waylaid by a man belonging to Carrick and his two sons. He had been bribed by the English, who, afraid to assail Bruce in his fastness, sought his overthrow by "slycht." Bruce was attended only by a page, and

Brunston Old Castle

Dalquharran Old Castle

Old Dailly Church
Photograph by A. Ritchie

was without arms, save his sword, which, as Barbour states, wherever he went it was his custom "about his hals to ber." When Bruce perceived the assassins coming upon him from their concealment, and recognised in the father a "sibman ner," that is a near relative of his own, he ordered them to remain where they were. The father urged his right as of kin to the king to be near his person, and "with fals wordis flechand" continued with his sons to advance. Barbour minutely describes the conflict that ensued. With a bow and a wire, which he borrowed from the page, he slew the elder of the assassins as he came forward—

> " He taisyt the wyr and let it fley,
> And hyt the fadyr in the ey,
> Till it rycht in the harnys ran ;
> And he backwart fell doun richt than."

The two sons, as they approached one after the other, with hatchet and spear, he slew with his sword. This, however, was only one of a series of personal adventures and perils, some of them still more astonishing.

LANDS GRANTED BY BRUCE.

But it would be outside our purpose to follow the stirring history any further. It only now remains for us to notice the grants of lands in our parish, originally made or confirmed by King Robert the Bruce.

1. We find him giving a grant of lands, doubtless for military services, to Fergus, son of Fergus. This is believed to have been the ancestor of the Fergussons of Kilkerran.

There is no record or tradition of any other residence in ancient times of the family except the present ruined Castle, which continued to be their residence till about 200 years ago, so that in all probability the lands thus gifted were in that neighbourhood.

2. We find again a charter from King Robert the Bruce dated 1324, 10 years after the Battle of Bannockburn, and another from Robert II., dated 1386, granting lands to the Cathcarts of Carleton. Whether these lands were at Killochan or Carleton in Colmonell does not appear, but there seems to have been a residence at Killochan as far back as 1477, although one can scarcely recognise the name under the strange garb which it wears. Hugh Cathcart of Kilzottane, in that year, is a witness to a charter in favour of Sir Alan de Cathcart.

3. As stated above, the Church of Dalmakeran (Dailly) was transferred along with its revenues from Paisley Abbey to the new Abbey of Crossraguel by King Robert the Bruce.

THE BLUE STONES OF OLD DAILLY.

Within the square enclosure attached to the north wall of Old Dailly Church, and which is probably the ancient and long disused tomb of the Boyds of Trochrague, lie two blue stones. For ages they have been used as tests of strength, the difficulty of the lift being increased by the smoothness and roundness of the stones. They appear, however, to have a history and associations which give them stronger claims on our interest. It may not be generally known that one of these stones is referred to as "a charter stone" in the notes to Sir Walter Scott's "Lord of the Isles." Sir Walter was indebted for his information to Mr. Joseph Train, of Newton-Stewart, author of some verses illustrative of Galloway and Ayrshire traditions, who, at his request, travelled in Ayrshire to collect materials for the notes to the poem.

The note referred to gives an account of certain benefactions by King Robert the Bruce in gratitude for having been cured of a disease, which was supposed to be leprosy, by drinking the waters of a medicinal spring near Ayr. He built houses round the well, which was called King's Case, for eight lepers, and assigned to them certain yearly donations, including eight bolls of oatmeal and £28, Scotch money, to each person, besides straw for the lepers' beds and to thatch their houses annually. The note then goes on to say:—"The Lepers' *Charter Stone* was a basaltic block, exactly the shape of a sheep's kidney, and weighing an Ayrshire boll of meal. The surface of this stone being as smooth as glass, there was not any other way of lifting it than by turning the hollow to the ground, there extending the arms along each side of the stone, and clasping the hands in the cavity. Young lads were always considered as deserving to be ranked among men when they could lift the blue stone of King's Case. It always lay beside the well till a few years ago,* when some English dragoons encamped at that place wantonly broke it, since which the fragments have been kept by the Freemen of Prestwick in a place of security. There is one of these Charter Stones at the village of Old Dailly, in Carrick, which has become more

* The Lord of the Isles" was published in 1815.

c

celebrated by the following event which happened only a
very few years ago * :—The village of New Dailly being now
larger than the old place of the same name, the inhabitants
insisted that the Charter Stone should be removed from
the old town to the new, but the people of Old Dailly were
unwilling to part with their ancient right. Demands and
remonstrances were made on each side without effect, till
at last man, woman, and child of both villages marched out,
and by one desperate engagement put an end to a war, the
commencement of which no person then living remem-
bered. Justice and victory, in this instance, being of the
same party, the villagers of the old town of Dailly now
enjoy the pleasure of keeping the ' blue stane' unmolested.
Ideal privileges are often attached to some of these stones.
In Girvan, if a man can set his back against one of the
above description, he is supposed not liable to be arrested
for debt; nor can cattle, it is imagined, be poinded as long
as they are fastened to the same stone. That stones were
often used as symbols to denote the right of possessing
land, before the use of written documents became general
in Scotland, is, I think, exceedingly probable. The
Charter Stone of Inverness is still kept with great care, set
in a frame, and hooped with iron, at the Market-place of
that town. It is called by the inhabitants of that district
Clach na Couddin. . . . While the famous marble chair
was allowed to remain at Scone, it was considered as the
Charter Stone of the Kingdom of Scotland." The
reference here is to the ancient stone in the Royal Palace
at Scone on which the Kings of Scotland were crowned,

* " The Lord of the Isles " was published in 1815.

and which was transferred to Westminster Abbey, and now forms part of the Coronation Chair of the Sovereigns of the United Kingdom. Whether there was anything about one or other, or both, of these two stones of the nature of a *Charter* or *Sanctuary* Stone cannot be known for certain ; but the fact that they were objects of so much contention shows that a more than ordinary value was attached to them—the tradition, no doubt, of something in the remote past.

They are said to have been originally placed within the church near the altar, where they would afford protection to criminals who took refuge beside them. Such sanctuaries or asylums for criminals are very ancient, their origin probably being the old Jewish cities of refuge, or the horns of the altar, at which there was safety for all but the wilful murderer. We find that Greek and Roman temples, especially the altars, were sometimes used for the same purpose. In the early ages of the Christian Church some of the Christian Emperors gave this privilege to certain churches, and bishops and monks improved upon the idea, extending the limits of asylum to churchyards and bishops' houses as well as to churches. In Scotland many churches enjoyed the right of sanctuary either from popular prestige or from royal authority, and some from their superior sanctity were considered to be safer than others. Our old church appears to have been one of those which possessed that privilege.

CHAPTER IV.

THREE HUNDRED YEARS AGO.

THERE is an old manuscript preserved in the Library of the Faculty of Advocates, Edinburgh, entitled a "History of the Kennedies." It is without date, but was evidently written near the beginning of the 17th century. The author is unknown, but whoever he was he seems to have been intimately connected with the leading actors in the scenes which he describes, and was evidently a strong supporter of the Bargany faction in the feuds of the period. The manuscript was published with notes and illustrations by Robert Pitcairn, W.S., in 1830. It is valuable as giving us a picture of the state of society in Carrick about the time of the accession of our King James to the English throne.

It is a very lurid picture that it presents to us. The history is very painful reading. The chief feature is the feud between the two great branches of the Kennedies, the Earls of Cassillis and the Earls of Bargany, and it is a dismal record of lawlessness and crime, of plots and conspiracies, of fightings and murders.

Without going into the question which seems to have been the origin, though not the only cause of this long-standing feud, the question of primogeniture, suffice it to say that the balance of evidence seems to be in favour of Bargany being the elder branch.

THE ORIGIN OF BARGANY.

The following is the old historian's account of the origin of the Bargany family. If not strictly accurate, we have no other reliable history to put in its place, and at all events it expresses the current belief of the time when the history was written.

As far back as the battle of Largs, in which Haco and the Danes were defeated, and which was fought in the year 1263, a Laird of Dunure ruled in Carrick from his rocky fastness by the sea which he had taken from the Danes. A hundred years later a Laird Maktaise appears upon the scene. The Laird of Dunure of that day, Sir John Kennedy, was anxious, according to the custom of the times, to get a sponsor or godfather for his newly born son, and asked Maktaise, who consented, and, having no family of his own, adopted the young Kennedy and made him his heir. Of that son came the house of Bargany.

"Friar Hew," a second son, was the first to bring the house of Bargany "to their preferment," and here we begin to get on to solid historical ground. He was destined for the office of a Friar, but a military career was more to his liking than chanting matins and vespers. Along with a kindred spirit, the Laird of Blairquhan, he crossed over to France, where he won the favour of King Charles VII., whom he assisted to fight the English in 1431,

and whom he accompanied on a crusading expedition to
the Holy Land. On his return he heard that his brother,
the Laird of Bargany, was dead, whereupon he took leave
of the King of France, who rewarded him handsomely for
his service, and gave him permission to wear the *fleur-de-lis*
on his coat of arms. Succeeding his brother, he was able,
by means of the treasure he brought from France, greatly
to extend the estate of Bargany, adding to it, among other
acquisitions, the lands of Ardstinchar, at the mouth of the
Stinchar, where he built a castle, the present ruin. If we
may judge from the nickname given to a grandson of Friar
Hew, viz., "Come with the penny," he seems to have
followed the example of his grandfather in enriching the
estate.

Let us take from the old chronicle a few outstanding
events, those more especially the scene of which was partly
in our own district.

BLACK BESSIE KENNEDY.

The ruins of Brounstone Castle, with which we are so
familiar, give but a faint idea of its extent and grandeur
300 years ago. At the time of our story the Castle was
occupied and the surrounding land possessed by a lady, the
aunt of Bargany by the father's side, and the aunt of the
tutor of Cassillis (the then Earl being in his minority), Sir
Thomas Kennedy of Culzean by the mother's side. She
was known by the name of Black Bessie Kennedy. She
was so called probably from her complexion, but if black
she may have been comely. At all events she had

attractions of some sort, for she was thrice married, and was now mourning her third husband, William Kennedy, "Baillie of Carrick." Before his death he had infeft her in his "Six pund land of Brounstone." There was, however, another claimant for the land. It appears that the Bailie had given the Earl of Cassillis—Gilbert, who roasted the Abbot—a previous infeftment of the same lands. The Earl, before his death in 1576, had infeft Lady Cassillis, Dame Mary Lyon, in these lands, and she being subsequently married to John, first Marquis of Hamilton, his Lordship opposed the claim of Black Bessie, and raised an action against her before the Lords of Session. Thereupon Bessie made over her right to Bargany, considering that he was better able to fight the battle, either on legal grounds or by force of arms, if that should be necessary. In lieu of Brunstone, Bargany gave her the six pound land of Newark, near Ayr. Then followed a "gude gangin' law plea." Decreet being at last given in favour of the Marquis, Bargany was turned out of Brunstone. The consequence was a new feud, this time between the two nephews, Bargany and Sir Thomas Kennedy, as to the custody of Black Bessie herself, and especially of her "assignations." Meantime, Bessie was staying with her nephew at Bargany, but the other nephew persuaded her to leave, and moved her to make him instead of Bargany her assignee, for she had considerable property left her by her first husband independent of Brunstone. Bargany was in a great rage, and an angry correspondence ensued. Two of the letters have been preserved, and they are choice specimens of the "polite" letter writing of the period. This

quarrel, more than anything else, was the cause of the
deadly feud between the two houses, which for many years
kept Carrick in a turmoil. In the above correspondence
there is a side light cast upon the amusements of the times.
It appears that Bargany played at golf, and that some time
before this he had got his nose smashed by a golf ball on
"the hills of Ayr," a disfiguration which Cassillis does not
hesitate to cast up to him in reply to a still coarser
personality. Golf, so fashionable at present, is a very
ancient Scottish game. There are traces of it at a much
earlier date. As far back as 1457, there is a Scottish
statute prohibiting it, on the ground that it discouraged
archery.

THE MURDER OF DRUMMOCHREEN.

Our readers will scarcely recognise the well-known name
under the uncouth spelling of the day, *Dromaquhryne.*
The name of the Lairds of Drummochreen was
Macalexander. The family is now extinct. After the
Reformation the greedy Scottish lairds made a grab not
only at the Church lands, but at the Church teinds or
tithes—the money, that is, left by pious persons in the old
times, and made by them payable by their lands for
religious purposes within the parish or parishes in which
they were interested. The lairds would have made a clean
sweep of the entire revenue of the Church but for one man,
John Knox. Thanks to his determination and firmness, a
proportion—small compared with the whole—of "the
patrimony of the Kirk," as he called it, was saved, and has

been handed down to us. It is *the property of the people of Scotland for religious purposes* in their several parishes, and is not to be lightly thrown away by them.

The teinds of this parish had belonged to the Abbey of Crossraguel, that is, the Abbot of Crossraguel drew the teinds, and in exchange supplied Christian ordinances to the parishioners in their Parish Church at Old Dailly. After the break up at the Reformation the Earl of Cassillis, among other acquisitions, had quietly entered into possession of the teinds payable by the lands of Drummochreen. The Earl had given a tack of the teinds to the Laird of Girvan Mains, who was one of the Kennedies, for " service." That is to say, Girvan Mains was to hold himself in readiness to follow the Earl when required, bringing with him so many horse and men. But the Laird of Girvan Mains had a little fighting to do on his own account, and wanted service himself, and so he sub-let his teinds to Laird Macalexander, on condition of receiving service from him. This arrangement, however, did not suit Drummochreen, who was "ane proud man." He wanted to hold the teinds direct from the Earl, and to transfer his " service " to him from his neighbour at Girvan Mains. He made this proposal to the Earl, who at once agreed to it. Thereupon Girvan Mains went to his residence, which was probably at Cassillis House, in a towering passion, to complain of his letting the teinds " to his ain man owre his heid," adding that " for ony gains he sall reap by that deed the same sall be but small." " Ye dare nocht find fault with him," said the Earl, " for if ye do," he added significantly, " we know were ye dwell." " An' he

byde by that deed," said the angry laird, " he sall repent of
the same, do for him wha lykit." " Ye dare nought steir
him for your craig. Gang your gait." Girvan Mains left
the Castle with two attendants, and waited for Drummochreen, who had also been at the Castle, at the " Moor
of Craigdow behind a knowe," near the point where their
roads home separated. When Drummochreen came up,
without any suspicion of danger, Girvan Mains and his two
men suddenly rushed upon him, " strak him with swords
on the head, and slew him." Although his brother and
another man were with him, they do not seem to have
struck a blow in his defence. Probably it was night, and
the darkness, and, at the same time, the suddenness of the
attack may account for it. A loose cairn of stones was
afterwards erected by the friends of the murdered man on
the spot where the bloody deed was done. It has been
kept up, and there it stands to this day. It is on the
north side of the old road leading past the hill of Craigdow,
and near the foot of the hill.

THE BATTLE OF AILSA CRAIG.

We now pass for a little from the history of the Kennedies
to take notice of a bit of Scottish history belonging to the
times of which we are writing, and of which the above
outlying portion of our parish was the scene.

In the end of the 16th century there lived and laboured
in Paisley a minister who was a bold, sturdy specimen of
the church militant, Mr. Andrew Knox. He could wield
the carnal sword as deftly as he could the spiritual sword,

and the enemy against whom he waged constant warfare
was the Pope of Rome. There was a great deal of panic
abroad in Scotland at this time, and that not all groundless,
about Popish plots. The Kirk was eager to hunt them out
and crush them, and there was no man who had a keener
scent for such game than the minister of Paisley. Five
years before the time to which we refer, he had done good
service in unearthing one of these plots. A discovery was
made, through Queen Elizabeth's ambassador at the
Scottish Court, that George Kerr, a Scottish Catholic
gentleman, was secretly passing into Spain with important
letters. Andrew was on his track at once. He managed
to get together a body of armed men, traced him to
Glasgow, thence to the Cumbraes, where he was seized
through the night immediately after he had got on board
the ship that was to carry him to the continent. Documents were found in his possession seriously compromising
the Popish Earls — Huntly, Angus, Errol, and others.
Among the rest there were blank papers signed by some
of them. Hence the plot is known in history as "The
Spanish Blanks." Kerr was put to the torture and confessed the conspiracy, the main branch of which was to
secure a footing for the invasion of Scotland by a Spanish
force.

In 1597, the year of Bargany's death, Barday of Ladyland,
in Renfrewshire, a Catholic baron, with a force of retainers,
seized and fortified Ailsa Craig and held it for the Spaniards,
who had promised to make a descent on that quarter.
Again the redoubtable Paisley minister was on the alert.
Girding on his sword, he set sail for the rock, with a few

equally daring associates, attacked the traitor, and reduced him to such straits that to avoid being taken alive, and probably to avoid compromising other lives by documents on his person, he rushed into the sea and was drowned. History does not record that the gallant services of Knox were acknowledged or rewarded either by the King or the Kirk.

CHAPTER V.

THE COVENANTERS OF DAILLY.

JOHN STEVENSON OF CAMREGAN.

ABOUT midway between Old Dailly Church and the present farm-steading of Camregan, on the south side of the road, and on a knoll now given up to the plough, there used to stand long ago a small farm-house called Midton of Camregan, or simply Camregan. More recently, and we believe within living memory, there was a school on the spot, and, later still, the dwelling-house of a retired school-master named Gilchrist, who was a great bird fancier, and had a large collection of feathered songsters. Within the farm-house was born, lived, and died one of the most remarkable men our parish has ever produced, John Stevenson. He was born in 1656, and died in 1729, aged 73. Nearly everything we know about him is from a pamphlet which he wrote in his old age, but which does not appear to have been published till after he died, as the title mentions the date of his death. It is in the form of an address to his children and grandchildren. There is " a preface in commendation," written by the Rev. William Cupples, minister of Kirkoswald. During Stevenson's early

45

life, up till his 25th year, Scotland was in the throes of the
covenanting struggle. The noble stand which our forefathers made, many of them at the cost of their lives, for
the cause of civil and religious liberty was associated with,
and was in a great measure the outcome of, a great national
awakening of spiritual life. No one can read the history
of these times without seeing that the usually unemotional
Scottish heart was stirred with extraordinary religious
fervour. The sayings and writings of those times show a
high-toned spirituality of feeling, such as we in these days
know nothing of. The young Camregan farmer was early
brought under strong religious impressions, and, after a
somewhat protracted struggle, at last gained a strong foot-
hold, and all through life seems to have lived on a high,
though somewhat sombre, level of religious experience.
He threw himself with eagerness in the cause of the
Covenant, and shared in the sufferings of the times. At
the age of 23 he was at the Battle of Bothwell Bridge,
where he had a narrow escape. He was often in hiding,
in haystacks, in Old Dailly Churchyard, on the hills above
his father's farm, and elsewhere, and with gratitude to God
he records many wonderful deliverances.

Though at one time quite common, John Stevenson's
"Soul strengthening and comforting cordial" is now
rarely to be met with. But while as a Dailly man John
Stevenson has a special claim upon us, the picture which
he gives of his life and spiritual experience has a far wider
than a merely local interest. It gives us a sample, so to
speak, of the inner life of the Covenanters, and brings
out strikingly wherein their great strength lay. If the

'experiences" recorded are thought to be occasionally
morbid or tinged with superstition, more especially in
reference to the Evil One, we must bear in mind that
these were defects characteristic of the religion of the
times, as any one can testify who has read the "Scots
Worthies."

An autumn day of the year 1678 seems to have been
memorable in his spiritual experience. The famous John
Welsh was preaching on Craigdow Hill to a large congregation, of which John Stevenson was one. His text was
2 Corinthians v., 20: "We beseech you, be ye reconciled
to God." Let Stevenson tell his experience in his own
words :—" In speaking from these words, the Lord helped
his servant not only to show what it was to be reconciled
to God but also earnestly to press reconciliation, and to
make a free, full, and pressing offer of Glorious Christ as
Mediator and Daysman and the great Peacemaker who
would make up the breach and bring about this much-
needed reconciliation,—I being fully convinced how greatly
I needed this reconciliation and Daysman, who is the only
way to the Father, I with all my heart and soul did cordially
and cheerfully make the offer welcome, and, without known
guile, did accept of and receive Glorious Christ on his own
terms in all his offices as Mediator, and did give myself away
to the Lord in a personal and perpetual covenant never to
be forgotten, accepting of God for my Lord, my God, my
Guide and my great reward after death—resolving, though
strange lords had the dominion over me, yet henceforth I
would be called by His name, whom I now avouched for
my only God and Lord, and resolved through grace to be

steadfast in His covenant till death; after which my soul was filled with joy and peace in believing—it was a joy unspeakable and glorious, having now got hope through grace that though He was angry yet now His anger was turned away and He was now become my salvation."

When the storm of persecution of the Covenanters had blown over, John Stevenson settled down quietly to his farm work, and spent the remainder of his days in peace and security in the midst of his family, and surrounded by scenes—the hillsides, Penquhapple glen, the old church-yard that were constant and vivid remembrances not only of the trials and sufferings, but of the merciful deliverances of byegone years. Having overcome his scruples in regard to joining in communion with the restored church, he was one of the most devout and earnest worshippers in the old church, and was no doubt a great support to the minister, Mr. Patrick Crawford, to whom he appears to have been deeply attached. On the occasion of the discontinuance of the church at Old Dailly as a place of worship and the erection of a church at New Dailly—not the present one but its predecessor—Mr. Crawford and his Kirk Session resolved to make an addition to the elder-ship. Naturally John Stevenson's name occurred to everybody, and along with three others he was made choice of by the Session—the congregation do not appear to have been formally consulted in the election—and their edicts having been duly served, they were ordained to the eldership in May, 1695, when John Stevenson was 39 years of age. The others were "The Laird of Carletoun,

William Lockhart in Drumlamford (Delamford), and John M'Gavin, Dailly." He died, according to his tombstone, on 17th March, 1729. No notice of his death is taken in the Session records. Old Dailly Churchyard, where "many a night he lay with pleasure, making a grave his pillow," is the spot where he now sleeps, waiting the resurrection morning. At the head of the grave there are two upright stones alongside of each other of different ages. There is also over the grave, and greatly overgrown with grass, a third stone, rough, unhewn, and unlettered, which probably was the original tombstone. On the older of the two above mentioned is the following inscription:—

> "Here lyes the
> corpse of John
> Stivnson, who
> died March 17,
> 1729, aged 73."

In his early religious experience there was a great deal of what the old Puritan divines would call "law work." But as a result of his long and sore "exercises" of soul he "digged deep," and the foundation was laid all the more firm and sure.

The most outstanding feature in his religious character was his prayerfulness. He was truly "a man of prayer." Fancy him continuing in prayer for his sick wife "for the most part" for forty-eight hours at a stretch! It was no uncommon thing for him to spend whole days in prayer. Imagine him with his broad blue bonnet and home-spun Sunday coat, with his well-thumbed Bible in his pocket

D

or under his arm, tramping over the hill on the early
morning of a week day to Kirkoswald Church—not the
present, but the old church in the graveyard, now a ruin—
where he would spend a whole day, sometimes two or
three days, in prayer and meditation, sleeping at the manse,
and " going into the church in the morning about sunrising
and not coming out till sunsetting, in the longest summer
day!" "It was my ordinary to set apart one day in the
month for fasting and humiliation, prayer and meditation,
and I found great quiet for it in the church at
Kirkoswald."

How could Stevenson find time for such frequent and
prolonged seasons of prayer? It must be borne in mind
that there was not the hurry-scurry in those days that there
is now. There was not the same dreadful competition.
Life was simpler. People's wants were fewer. While there
was need for toil in the class to which John Stevenson
belonged, there was less need for that toil being all-
engrossing. And if covetousness—the eager craving for
more than people really need—found a place, as it has
always done, in human hearts, we may be sure it found no
place in such a heart as that of the Camregan farmer.
There are no signs in his nature of the choking " thorns."
A man, even a working man, might thus in those days be
able, without harm to the worldly welfare of himself or
family, to take a day or more from his work for any object
on which his heart was set. And if John Stevenson was in
danger of neglecting his farmwork or his family, he had
many texts in his mind from the Book he knew and loved
so well which would be sure to keep him right.

JOHN SEMPLE OF ELDINGSTON.

As John Stevenson survived for many years the perils of
the times, he was not a Martyr in the ordinary sense, but
there were others belonging to our parish who can be
classed among "the noble army," having sealed their
testimony with their blood. The name of one of these
stands at the head of this paper.

Let us first take a glance at the times. It was the year
1685. The night of persecution was now at its darkest.
What with the Privy Council in Edinburgh, with its
bloody scaffold in the Grassmarket, with its boots and
thumbscrew, and Graham of Claverhouse and his dragoons
galloping up and down in the west country shooting and
capturing them, and with no hope now of taking the field
against their oppressors, the Covenanters were in an evil
plight and might well say, " We are killed all the day long ;
we are accounted as sheep for the slaughter."

In the month of May, 1684, a Royal Proclamation had
been issued with a roll of nearly 2,000 persons, who are
described as "fugitives from law," and denouncing pains
and penalties against them as "rebellious and unnatural
subjects." This proscription roll is given in Wodrow's
History. There are on it 13 names of persons belonging
to our parish, viz. : — Maclarchan, son to Andrew
Maclarchan, officer in Bargeny (his Christian name is
not mentioned. He is probably the same person as the
Thos. M'Lorgan who was buried in the same grave as John
Semple in Old Dailly Churchyard, and who was shot,
according to the inscription, " uncertain by whom ") ; David

Kennedy, son to John Kennedy, in Currow (Curragh) of
Bargeny; John Semple, in Eldinstone; John Stevenson,
younger, in Cambregan; Thomas German there; Thomas
Maccubin, in Blair; John Macalexander, younger of
Drummochrin, forfeited; Gilbert German, weaver, in
Drummochrin; Hugh Purdin, miller, in Drummochrin;
John Bryce, in Drumillan; John MacIlraith, in Farden;
John MacLean, in Dobiston; Thomas Mackskimming, in
Auchneicht.

Dr. Cunningham in his History of the Church of Scotland says of this period that "it was the most melancholy
period in the history of the Church. The furnace into
which the children of the Covenant were to be cast was
heated seven times. . . . No one was safe from the violence
of a brutalised soldiery. Their form of process was very
simple and very brief. A few questions generally decided
their verdict. Do you think the slaughter of the Archbishop (Sharp) was murder? Was the rising at Bothwell
rebellion? Will you take the Test Oath? Will you take
the Abjuration Oath? Will you pray for the King? The
peasantry were generally too conscientious to tell a lie,
often too scrupulous to take an oath, and sometimes too
simple to understand the meaning of the questions which
were put; and the answers which they gave determined
whether they were to live or die. Sentence being pro-
nounced, a file of soldiers with loaded carbines carried it
into instant execution. The victim was asked to draw his
bonnet over his eyes, and the next moment he fell dead or
dying to the ground. Thus many were shot by the wayside
in the fields, at their own door."

Two hundred years ago, on the lower slopes of Hadyet, there stood on the bank of a burn that whimples through a little glen overhung with oaks and alders, and at a distance of about two hundred yards to the south of where Maxwelton farm house now stands—a humble bigging called Eldingston, or Eldington. The field in which it stood used to go by the name of "Eldingston Park," but it is also called the "Dam Park." There are now no traces of the house, but when the field was ploughed many years ago, cinders and other indications of a human dwelling were turned up on the spot. At the time we speak of, the house and the small farm attached were tenanted by John Semple. He was married, and had a family of young children. John had cast in his lot with the Covenanters. When the Sabbath day came round his steps were directed, not to the Parish Church at Old Dailly to worship under the Rev. Thomas Skinner, the Episcopal minister, but to the neighbouring hill, where, on what is called the Sauchhill, there was a regular "conventicle," probably of wood and turf. And when any of the outed ministers were to preach in the dining-room of Killochan Castle, or on Craigdow Hill, John's broad bonnet was to be seen among the crowd that gathered from far and near. He and his wife were a kindly, hospitable couple, though their means were humble. Many of "the sufferers" from the water of Stinchar, or from the more distant wilds of Galloway, knew the track over the brow of Hadyet or round the Camphill which led to Eldingston, where they were sure of a warm welcome and a friendly crack by the ingle about the common cause. John was otherwise a quiet and inoffensive man. He does not appear to have gone with John Stevenson to Bothwell Bridge. He seems never to have been accused of having borne arms. Still, from his hospitality to the persecuted and his frequenting conventicles, he became a marked man, and his name had appeared in the "Proclamation and List of Fugitives," published in May, 1684. Knowing that Cornet Douglas and his soldiers were hunting for Covenanters in the district, and hearing of their bloody doings elsewhere, John must have known that his life hung by a slender thread. But it was as much the thought of his wife and bairns as of himself that made him lie awake at night, or start, fancying that he heard in the croon of the burn or the rustle of the trees the steps of the red coats.

The then laird of Kilkerran, Alexander Fergusson, who at that time appears to have had his residence at Moorston, and who was married to a daughter of the Bishop of Galloway, was unfavourable to the cause of the Covenant. One day, it was in the month of April, 1685, he betook himself to Blairquhan Castle, and laid information against John Semple before Lieutenant Dundas, then in command of the garrison stationed there.

A party of soldiers, under the orders of Cornet Douglas, was dispatched about sunset, Alexander Fergusson being their guide. He first conducted them to his own house at Moorston, where he entertained them hospitably to supper. Starting about the middle of the night, when they thought their victim was sure to be at home, in the course of half an hour they were at Eldingston, and immediately surrounded the house. Semple, with an ear habitually quickened by a sense of danger, at once heard their tread and whisperings. His only chance of escape was a small window, and while he was struggling to get through, and was half out and half in, five or six muskets were levelled at him, and in an instant there was a mangled corpse in the window, and on the floor a crushed and broken-hearted widow with her fatherless children clinging to her in a frenzy of grief and terror.

The murderers now retired to the barns of Bargany to refresh themselves after their night's work, and, according to the narrative, drank and caroused there all next day. Were there some of the party making desperate efforts in this way to drown the voice of an innocent man's blood crying out of the ground? Perhaps there was something of this inner disquietude underneath the reply given by Alexander Fergusson to a woman in the neighbourhood, who, a few days after, upbraided him for the part he had taken in the murder of an innocent man, who had left a wife and four or five shiftless children behind him. "He scornfully replied that it was a piece of kindness done to her and them, since her husband, with those he entertained, would have eaten up all they had."

The body of John Semple was reverently laid in the grave at Old Dailly Churchyard. At or about the same time another Dailly man had met the same fate, viz., Thomas M'Clorgan, mentioned in the roll of fugitives given above. We know nothing of the circumstances of his martyrdom. Whether or not it occurred at the same time as Semple, they were laid in the same grave. An old flat stone with an inscription scarcely decipherable covers their grave. And at the head of the grave, in the year 1825, there was erected by public subscription a memorial obelisk, sometimes called "The Martyrs' Stone," containing a copy of the old inscription, which is as follows :—"Here lies the corpse of John Semple, who was shot by Kilkerran at command of Cornet James Douglas; also, here lies Thomas M'Clorgan, who was shot (uncertain by whom), for their adherence to the Word of God and the covenanted work of Reformation, 1685." The inscription does not quite agree with Wodrow's account, which states that Semple was shot by a number of pieces discharged simultaneously, and it seems a very unlikely thing that the Laird of Kilkerran should have been under the orders of a Cornet or Lieutenant like a common soldier. The probability is that there is a little exaggeration in the inscription. The friends of the Martyrs, in their natural indignation at such crimes, were eager to pillory somebody for them, and perhaps put upon the stones they erected over their graves the names of persons as their murderers who had only been act and part, and this they did the more readily if these persons had otherwise incurred odium from their hostility to the cause.

GEORGE MARTIN.

Two hundred years ago what we now call Old Dailly was the centre of the population of the parish. At New Dailly, then called Milcavish, there was a corn mill with a house for the miller and one or two other houses. But

Old Dailly, which was then simply called Dailly, was the main centre of the population. When the Parish Church was removed in 1690 to New Dailly, *that* gradually became the centre of the population, as it is the centre of the parish locally, and Old Dailly began to fall into decay. But, at the time we refer to, it was a place of some importance, situated on the Penquhapple burn at the point where the public road crossed the burn by a bridge, the remains of which may still be seen. There, embosomed among trees, stood the Parish Church, even then hoary with antiquity, with its two belfry towers, the eastern surmounted by a cross and surrounded by its old churchyard. And further down the burn, on the opposite side of the road, was the modest and unpretentious manse. We may picture to ourselves the village as standing on both sides of the road—the old road—and composed of rows or clusters of thatch houses, with an inn, a smithy, a wright's shop, the school and schoolmaster's house, and the usual village population.

One of the most important, if not *the* most important, man in the village at the time we are speaking of, and a man held in honour not only for his position, but for his Christian character, was George Martin, the schoolmaster. In addition to teaching, he held other two offices, those of "reidar and notar." After the Reformation, when there was a difficulty in supplying parishes with regular ministers, "readers," corresponding very much to our "lay missionaries," were appointed; and it is remarkable, as showing the importance of our parish in those days, that, while neighbouring parishes were only supplied with readers,

Dailly had both a minister and a reader. Whether this arrangement continued without interruption down to the times we refer to we do not know, but it appears that at this time there was a reader as well as a minister, and George Martin held the office. The minister was the Rev. Thomas Skinner, whose pulpit Bible is still in existence. We know very little about him, but he seems to have been one of those Episcopal curates who were called "dumb dogs that could not bark," rather than go to hear whom many of our forefathers were ready to lay down their lives on the hillside or on the scaffold. It seems likely, therefore, that the well-known learning and piety of the schoolmaster, who was a true son of the Covenant, were taken advantage of by the Covenanting parishioners, and that, at the risk of his life, he conducted service for their benefit in the wooden conventicle on the neighbouring Sauch Hill, unless when John Welsh, or some other of the outed ministers, was at hand.

In addition to his other duties, Martin found time to discharge the duties of a "notar," or notary. He was a kind of country lawyer, and though his "practice" could not be very great, the mere fact of its being worth while for a man to practice as a notary in Old Dailly shows that the village was at this time, and probably had long been, a place of importance with a larger population than gathered in most country villages. Whether or not we can call it, as some have called it, a "borough," it might perhaps deserve the name of a "town."

Nearly everything we know of George Martin is derived from the brief account of his trial in the Justiciary records, and his dying testimony contained in "The Cloud of Witnesses"—a work which contains the dying testimonies of many of the martyrs of the Covenant, and which was first published in 1714, though the materials were in preparation for many years before that. We get, however, a glimpse, but it is only a glimpse, of him in the pages of Wodrow some years previous to his apprehension, as follows :—The then proprietor of Bargany—Lord Bargany —was favourable to the cause of the Covenant. He was one of those "Westland gentry" who stoutly refused to sign the bond, one object of which was to root out conventicles. He was on very friendly terms with Martin, and if he did not worship at the Sauchhill, he is known to have sent encouraging letters by the hands of a servant to the congregation worshipping there, as appears from the indictment on the occasion of his trial. It also appears from the same source that he had oral or written communications of a very compromising nature with George Martin, which somehow had leaked out, we may believe, through no fault of Martin—to the effect that they, the Covenanters, would never succeed so long as the Duke of Lauderdale—the President of the Council—was alive, and that a hundred men could do more by assaulting him in his house at Lethington than all they could do beside.

In 1679, the year of the battle of Bothwell Bridge, Martin was apprehended. We know that after the battle Claverhouse and his dragoons were in this district making prisoners of those who had been, or who were, suspected of being at Bothwell Bridge, and who refused to accept of the indemnity, thumbscrews and lighted matches between the fingers being used by them as instruments of torture to elicit evidence. Although it does not appear that George Martin was at the battle, still his connection with the conventicle rendered him a marked man, and he was apprehended. Along with a batch of other prisoners, he was sent to Edinburgh, and he was actually kept in prison —we do not know where—for four years and four months without a trial. During this long period he was occasionally in irons night and day, and during winter without fire. The marvel is that he survived to be at last tried.

The record of his trial, as it stands on the Justiciary books, is dated 11th February, 1683. "Being interrogated if he owns the King to be lawful King, and will pray for him, declares he will not say he disowns him, but owns all lawful authority according to the Word of God. He will not answer whether Bothwell Bridge be rebellion, but says if it was a rebellion against God, it was rebellion; if not, it was not rebellion. He will not subscribe. Being interrogated if the late King's death was murder, declares they that did it had more skill than he; refuses to call it murder, and says he does not think it pertinent to give a declaration anent it."

On the sole ground of these answers, and without the examination of a single witness, George Martin was sentenced to be hanged.

On the 22nd of February he was led forth to the scaffold in the Grassmarket. The picture of him on the last day of his life which his dying address gives us is that of a man calm and peaceful, for whom the Grassmarket and its scaffold have no terrors—grieved only about the sins of the world and the Church. "He refused his life, being an engrained Whig," says the old chronicler, Fountainhall, with a sneer (the name Whig being the contemptuous epithet given to the Covenanters in those days by their enemies). But there was something else, something deeper and nobler than Whiggism, engrained into the soul of the Dailly schoolmaster.

JOHN LORD BARGANY.

We have already mentioned the name of John Lord Bargany in our account of George Martin, the schoolmaster. Although not so closely identified with the Covenanting struggle as those whose names we have recorded, his connection with it was such that our sketches under the above heading would not be complete without some reference to him.

It was he who built the present mansion - house of Bargany, with the exception of the drawing-room wing, which is a later addition. The old house, in which he lived the greater part of his life, is thus described by Mr. William Abercrummie, Episcopal minister of Maybole, who wrote a "Description of Carrick" 200 years ago :— "Next to Brunstowne, in the midst of a forest rather than wood, stands, in a low ground near the brink of the river, the old castle of Bargeny, on the south syde of Girvan; which is ane argument of the sometime greatnesse of that family, being a hudge great lofty tower in the center of a quadrangular court that had on each of three corners fyne well-built towers of freestone, four story high."

He first comes before us in 1678, as one of the noblemen and gentlemen in Ayrshire who stoutly refused to sign the "Bond" by which those signing became responsible for their tenants keeping clear of the "rebels," and became bound under pains and penalties to have themselves no intercourse with them, to have no connection with conventicles, and, generally, to do all in their power to stamp out the movement. Among others in Ayrshire who refused were the Earls of Cassillis and Loudoun, the Lords Montgomery, Cochran, and Cathcart. They were denounced as "King's rebels," and from that day Lord Bargany could not but feel that the sword was hanging over his head.

Later on his courage and constancy to the oppressed cause were put to a further test. A host of 10,000 men, of whom 6,000 were Highlanders, rude caterans accustomed to plunder and murder, were sent into the Western counties to crush the Presbyterians. We may note in passing that the Gaelic spoken by these men was quite understood, perhaps too well understood, by the people of Ayrshire and Galloway, an evidence that the Celtic language which at one time prevailed in the West, and which still survives in names of places, had not at that time become extinct. A committee of the Privy Council accompanied the host, to point out to them the victims of oppression. The atrocities committed by the soldiers are almost incredible. A general feeling of indignation was aroused even among many who were not in full sympathy with the Covenant, and when Bargany was ordered to meet with others who were appointed by the Council "Commissioners of Excise," and who were ordained to fix on the rates at which provisions should be sold to the soldiers, and see that the provisions were conveyed to the garrisons, he met the order by a firm and bold refusal.

We are not, therefore, surprised to learn that, on the fresh outburst of persecuting fury occasioned by the battle of Bothwell Bridge, Bargany was seized and imprisoned under the charge of having been concerned in the rising. Private malice appears to have been working behind the scenes, for the times gave scope and opportunity for the revenging of private quarrels. Bargany, like other men in those troublous times, had enemies, who did their best to rake up evidence against him, and were not at all scrupulous in their methods. Thomas Cunningham of Mount Greenan was induced, it is said, by "vile methods," to come forward and give evidence in regard to Bargany's connection with Bothwell Bridge, and communicating with Mr. Welsh, one of the most prominent of the outed ministers. In the winter of 1679 he was imprisoned in Blackness, one of the king's castles on the Firth of Forth. He was examined by a committee, and his declaration was taken.

Meantime, many a secret conclave is being held among the conspirators; and one after another of those who had been present from this district at Bothwell Bridge—for then, as always, there were tares mixed with the wheat—were induced to promise they would swear falsely at the trial that Bargany had sent them. Depositions of the most damaging nature were carefully drawn up in their name.

It appears, however, that the witnesses could not be induced to come forward, notwithstanding the bribe held out to them of a share of the fair lands of Bargany in the event of the charge being found proven and the estate confiscated. In consequence the trial had to be postponed day after day. As the day came the witnesses "could not bring themselves to swear against the innocent man, and plainly refused to do it."

Bargany now appealed to the king, and His Majesty was induced to stop the process against him. The king's letter bears that "he had received a petition from the Lord Bargany representing his father's (the first Lord Bargany) loyalty and sufferings, asserting his innocence of the crimes he is indicted for and attesting God thereupon, and His Majesty requires him to be liberate under sufficient caution to appear in order to trial if hereafter sufficient proof of his guilt be found." Accordingly by an order dated 3rd June, 1680, the Council command the Governor of the Castle of Edinburgh to set him at liberty.

After he was set at liberty, he obtained proofs of the conspiracy against him, and he was quite prepared in 1681 to produce his evidence before Parliament, but, as the investigation was going to implicate persons of high rank, the Duke of York interposed to stop further proceedings. But he had another task on hand during the same year. When he exchanged the prison cells of Blackness and Edinburgh for the free air of his own beautiful Bargany, he completed the building of the new house which had probably been begun before his imprisonment. The following is Abercrummie's description of it—"The new house lately built, after the modern fashion, stands upon a higher ground southward of the Old Castle, which furnished materials both for founding and finishing of the new house. It is a mighty commodious house, and if any make a greater show and appearance, yet it has the advantage of them for contrivance and accommodation. It is flanked to the south with gardens very pretty, and has orchards lying westward of it."

Bargany appears now to have thoroughly made his peace with the Government, for not only was he released from his "bond of compearance," but three years afterwards, or in 1684, he was appointed one of the King's Commissioners in Ayrshire, acting under instructions to proceed against the Covenanters. But if he turned against his former friends, he helped afterwards to secure for the nation the fruit of their struggles and sufferings, for in 1689 he threw himself heartily into the cause of the Revolution, and raised in its service a force of 400 foot. That is the last glimpse we get of him. He died on 25th May, 1693.

The title of Lord Bargany has long been extinct. The last Lord Bargany died young on 28th March, 1736, and was buried in Holyrood Abbey, Edinburgh. He appears to have been a man of great accomplishments. A poet of the day, Hamilton of Bangor, speaks of him as:

> "Kind Bargany, faithful to his word,
> Whom Heaven made good and social though a lord,
> The cities viewed of many languaged men."

E

THE LAIRD OF DRUMMOCHREEN.

About a mile above the village, on the north bank of the river, and near the present march between Kilkerran and Dalquharran, there stood at the time we are writing of, the fair mansion of Drummochreen. Nothing now remains but a plain bit of ivy-clad wall with a small window in it. The ground beside it has been kept sacred from the plough, and to the north are a number of ancient trees, beeches, Scotch firs and planes, some of them indicating the approach, which seems to have been from that side. We are fortunate in having a description of the house and its immediate surroundings as they appeared 200 years ago—at or about the time of the persecution—from the pen of the Rev. Mr. Abercrummie, the Maybole curate, from whom we have formerly quoted. He waxes quite eloquent over the scene. He describes it as "a most lovely thing." The house, though not showy, was most convenient and commodious, "fit to lodge the owners and his neighbours." There were extensive outhouses. There were gardens, orchards, and ponds with all sorts of fish, a waulk mill, a corn mill, and artisans and tradesmen of different sorts, so that the banks of the river at this spot, now so silent and deserted, 200 years ago presented a scene of busy life and industry.

We cannot help thinking there was a quiet sneer under the curate's words when he spoke of the Laird as having a house that could "not only lodge himself but his neighbours." For it was a fact that the Laird—John Macalexander—was given to hospitality towards the persecuted Covenanters, and he was specially charged with having harboured outed ministers, and when the "Highland host" was sent into the West in 1678 to overawe and crush the Covenanters, he had to pay dearly for it. In that year the Laird of Glenlyon, at the head of 800 Highlanders, had been let loose upon the Parish of Straiton. There was one man who welcomed the invasion, and that was the curate of Kirkoswald. Many of the curates remained quiet, and took no active part in the persecution, and the Dailly curate, the Rev. Thomas Skinner, was one of these; but others gave information, and generally made themselves active tools in the hands of the enemies of the Covenant. The curate of Kirkoswald was particularly zealous. No sooner did the troops enter Ayrshire than he went to the commanding officer, and prevailed on him to send a detachment to Kirkoswald; and it was by his information that quarters were ordered, and many houses, whose owners had incurred the wrath of this meek apostle by harbouring the sufferers in any way, had some of these wild, rude caterans from the hills billetted on them at "free quarters." John Macalexander was one of these, and for a time the accommodation and resources of his establishment were strained to the utmost. And, besides giving free quarters to the soldiers, and submitting to all their rudeness, he had to pay a fine of 80 pounds Scots.

The punishment, however, does not seem to have taken much effect in the way of a warning. In 1679 was fought the battle of Bothwell Bridge, so disastrous to the cause of the Covenant. Those who had been there, or who were suspected of having been there, were proceeded against with the utmost rigour. A number of Ayrshire lairds were indicted, and John was one of them. None of them seemed to have answered the indictment, and they were all "forfeited," and, when taken, ordained to be executed as traitors. Wodrow, the historian, adds that from the papers connected with the case which he saw, it was by no means proved that Macalexander was at Bothwell Bridge. Still he seems to have thought it safer not to trust himself to a trial, and continued in hiding. How he managed to escape history does not tell. For years the sword seemed to have hung over his head, as in 1684 his name appears in the "List of Fugitives," that is hose who had been at Bothwell, or had harboured or resetted any who had been there, to be proceeded against as traitors, if they failed to take the bond or test within a certain time. After his name occurs the ominous word "forfeited." Besides the Laird, Drummochreen has the honour of giving other two names to the list, viz., Gilbert German, the weaver, and Hugh Purdin, the miller, who, if they had not been at the battle themselves, could tell if they chose something about the secret whereabouts of some who had been or were suspected of having been there.

QUINTIN KENNEDY OF DRUMMELLAN.

Just opposite Drumburle, a little higher up the river, on the south side, there stood in those days another mansion-house called Drummellan, belonging to a branch

of the Kennedies. A portion of the house, which some
time previously had been destroyed by fire, was in
existence at the beginning of the century, but the property
having passed into the hands of Kilkerran, the stones
were removed to build wings to the present house. At the
time of the persecution the Laird was Quintin Kennedy
who was married to Jean Boyd of Penkill. He was a
soldier, and had been appointed one of the Commissioners
for ordering the militia of Carrick, and, at the same time,
was captain of a troop of dragoons. In that position the
Royalist party naturally expected him to join in the
raid against the Presbyterians. But he stoutly refused,
and although there was a standing feud between him
and his neighbour at Drummochreen about a mill-dam,
concerning which there had been a "gude ganging
law plea," he refused to follow the example of others
who took advantage of the times to gratify their private
malice. One at least of his people was suspected, and
his name, John Bryce, appears on the black "List of
Fugitives" above referred to. So anxious were the
Royalists to gain Drummellan's valuable aid in crushing
the Covenanters, that he was waited upon by two of
them, both personal friends of his own, viz., Sir Archibald
Kennedy of Culzean, and the other no less a personage
than Graham of Claverhouse, "the bloody Claverse," the
arch-enemy of the Covenant, at whose door lay so much
of the Covenanters' blood. The Laird's reply to their
solicitations must have made Claverhouse wince. "No!"
he said proudly, "I will serve the king in the field, but I
will not be his executioner."

CONVENTICLES.

The year 1660 was a dark year for Scotland. In that year occurred the restoration of Charles II. Episcopacy was once more in the ascendant. The Covenant was declared treasonable, and ministers who would not acknowledge the authority of the bishops were forced to resign their livings. Their places were filled by " Curates," for the most part ill-educated, and many of them immoral in their lives.

Many of the outed ministers who had left their manses had not left their parishes, and continued to preach, though no longer in the Parish Church. Many of them travelled about the country preaching wherever they had an opportunity. The people flocked to hear from their lips the gospel which persecution only made dearer to them. These gatherings were called "conventicles." Sometimes they were held in the halls of mansion houses where the laird was favourable to the Covenant, sometimes in barns or in rude buildings of timber and turf, but latterly they were most frequently held in the open air on a hillside or in some sequestered spot among the hills surrounded by heights on which sentries could be posted to give warning of the approach of the dragoons. Sometimes these conventicles lasted for several days, many of the people sleeping in their plaids in some sheltered nook or cave.

As might have been expected in such a covenanting district as this, there were many such gatherings in our parish and the immediate neighbourhood. We know of

four different places where conventicles were held more
or less frequently, three of them within the parish, and
the one mentioned last just over the march between Dailly
and Kirkoswald, viz.—the Sauchhill, the dining-room of
Killochan Castle, Lane, and Craigdow Hill.

THE SAUCHHILL CONVENTICLE.

The range of hills which serve as a rampart to our valley
on the south is cleft in twain by a hollow at the bottom
of which is a wooded and picturesque ravine through which
flows the Penquhapple Burn. This spot appears to have
been a favourite hiding-place during the persecuting times.
On the right bank, a short distance below where Penkill
Castle nestles on the brink of the ravine, is a cave, of
no great depth, high up on the rocks, called Bennan's
Cave, which tradition points out as the hiding-place of
the Covenanter, George Maclure of Bennan, in the Parish
of Barr, whose name honourably appears on the "List
of Fugitives."

The point where the broken ridge rises gently from this
deep depression into the hills that extend towards the sea
beyond Girvan is called the Sauchhill, and somewhere
on the slope of that hill, and thus convenient to Old Dailly,
which as we have seen was then the centre of the population
of the parish, stood in the days we are writing of, a humble
wooden shed, roofed probably with turf or heather, or both
combined. This was the famous Sauchhill Conventicle—
for the name, like the word church, was applied to the

building as well as to the people. There are no traces of it now, and not even tradition can tell where it stood.

Thither, especially when the news spread that John Welsh or some of the more famous hill preachers had come to the district, the people flocked from far and near, shepherds from the hills, farmers from the water of Stinchar or Assil, fisher folk from Girvan and along the shore, and a sprinkling from the Castle as well as the cottage, the men in their blue bonnets and plaids and hodden gray, the women in home-spun shawls and hoods, mothers leading their children or carrying babies to be baptized.

We have reason to believe that the Sauchhill Conventicle was at times something more than a meeting for worship and hearing a sermon. The conventicle appears sometimes to have become a conference or convention, at which communications were received and read, and matters discussed affecting the common cause. At these meetings George Martin, the schoolmaster, the martyr of the Grassmarket, seems to have been prominent, perhaps at times presiding. It will be recollected that it was at one of these Sauchhill Conventions that the compromising letter from John Earl of Bargany was read, which formed one of the charges against him at his trial.

On 7th February, 1678, at the time when the Highland host was ravaging the district as if it were a conquered country, a meeting of the Committee of Privy Council was held at Ayr. Though not a member of council, the Earl of Cassillis, as Bailie Principal of Carrick, was present. One of the first things brought before them was the existence of two "meeting houses" in Carrick, that on Sauchhill and another, the locality of which is not known. Cassillis was at once ordained to "raze them to the ground or to destroy or burn them, and to make a strict and exact inquiry into the persons who built them or had been actors and abettors thereof, and whose ground they were built on." Some time before this the committee had issued an order for all persons to give up their arms, noblemen and gentlemen of quality having license to wear swords only, and Cassillis was enjoined to carry out this order from which he himself was not exempt. When he received this further order from the council he naturally demurred in his comparatively defenceless position, and urged that at least he should be allowed a force of soldiers or the assistance of some of the neighbouring gentlemen. This was refused. Would they allow him then to have some of his own arms back, "in case a rabble of the country people or a tumultuary crowd were it but of women in defence of their meeting houses might hinder or affront him." But neither would this be allowed. The Earl was going on to make further remonstrances when one of the members of committee, a friend of his own, whispered in his ear that there was but a hair's breadth between him and imprisonment if he made any further difficulty. A glance at the stern faces around the council table confirmed the warning, and the Earl bowed a silent acquiescence.

But we have not heard the last of the Sauchhill Conventicle. The Earl must have had personal enemies on the Committee of Council, as they seemed bent on driving him

further and further to the wall. He reported that he had
demolished the meeting houses, and razed them to the
ground. It was true it had been done, but not that he
had done it. But my Lords were not satisfied. They
issued a new warrant, commanding him " to bring back the
cut timber of the meeting houses to the same place where
they were built and to cause cut it in pieces and there to
burn the same to ashes," which accordingly he caused to
be done.

THE LANE'S CONVENTICLE.

About 100 yards on the left hand side of the road to
Barr, near the Old Lanes Toll, and at the point where the
road begins to wind down toward the Stinchar, stands an
upright dark grey granite boulder called "Peden's pulpit."
It is five feet six inches broad at the base, two
feet five inches in thickness, and five feet six inches
in height. It is in appearance a sort of irregular
pyramid. On the top, which slopes towards the
south, a hole is drilled in the stone to the depth of
an inch and one-third in diameter. There are also two
depressions cut in the stone near this hole, and altogether
these may have been designed for fixing a bookboard.
The slope of the bookboard being towards the south would
enable the preacher, on the supposition that the stone was
used for a pulpit, to have his back to the sun, and he would
have the prevailing wind in his favour for carrying the
sound to the congregation scattered over the knolls and
ridges in front of him. On the south side of the stone

lies a flat irregular slab about a foot in thickness, on which
the minister is supposed to have stood. Peden's pulpit,
which is on the estate of Knockgerran, was re-inspected by
the late Mr. Daniel Mackie, whose antiquarian tastes and
knowledge are well known, and it is to him that we are
indebted for the above description. In examining the flat
slab Mr. Mackie was surprised to notice what had escaped
observation before, traces of an incised Latin cross, that is
the cross with the upright longer than the transverse.
This of course carries us to an age away beyond Peden and
the Covenanters. It evidently belongs to Roman Catholic
times. Could there have been a small chapel on the spot?
It is needless for us to speculate further. There it lies,
with its secret too well guarded. And yet it tells a tale.
Long ages ago, in the primeval times, that big boulder had
its home in the granite rocks above what is now Loch
Doon. It was the time when perpetual snow covered our
mountains and ice filled our valleys. One day it fell
crashing upon the glacier below, which gradually and
slowly working its way towards the sea brought it down to
where it now lies, and left it there to fulfil its future
mission. It was the time when on the other side of the
ridge to the north, and in the hollow through which the
Penquhapple flows in its upper reaches, a big *moraine* or
kaime was deposited also through glacial agency. That
is the first chapter in the story which this book of stone
tells. The second presents us with a picture, though dim
and hazy, of a time when another winter reigned on our
hillsides and valleys—the winter of religious formalism and
superstition—yet not altogether barren and desolate. It

is the age of crosses and other symbolisms—of outward forms and ceremonies. And now the third chapter opens. A grave and solemn man with bared head and hair flowing in the breeze stands beside that stone. Before and around is a great gathering of earnest worshippers. Sentries have been posted on Auchensoul Hill and the other heights around. The Psalm has been sung and carried far on the breeze. The prayer—an earnest wrestling with God in which the woes of Scotland and her persecuted Church are not forgotten—has been offered, and then follows the sermon, earnest and homely, with a strong evangelical ring, rousing and startling in its appeals.

Verily this is a new era which the third chapter of the stoney book brings before us. The Covenanting minister standing with his foot on the symbolical cross is emblematic. Romish and Episcopal symbolisms and ceremonials are under his feet. The Covenanters' worship may be bare even to baldness, but surely it is more of the worship in spirit and in truth. And for the worship and word of God they are there at fearful risks. The *symbolical* cross may not be there, but the *real* cross is there held up before the minds and hearts of all men. And the cross of suffering too was there or was not far away. And these men and women had taken it up, and chosen to suffer affliction with the people of God rather than worship against their consciences, and with dragoons quartered at Blairquhan, Girvan, and elsewhere, and scouring the country, they knew they might have a dreadful account to give for their presence there that day. And the minister's blood might be deepening the purple of the heather before that sun set, or he might be on his way to the scaffold in the Grass-market in Edinburgh.

This old gray stone, whose silent story we have been trying to extract, tradition calls Peden's pulpit. We know that the well-known wandering Covenanter and prophet frequented this district. We know further that he stayed and preached one night in a house in the neighbourhood, viz., Penjarroch. The house is no longer in existence, but the traces of it can be seen about a mile nearer the Stinchar down the glen, at the head of which the stone stands. The site is marked by an aged sycamore tree. There is thus every reason to believe the testimony of tradition that Peden preached, perhaps repeatedly, here, and the arrangements for a bookboard and footboard seem to point to the conclusion that the stone was frequently used as a pulpit, and that conventicles were often held on the spot.

THE KILLOCHAN CONVENTICLE.

The Covenanting movement was not confined to one class. It was no doubt essentially a popular movement. It sprang from and derived its strength from the mass of the people. Still there were not a few of the Lairds who threw in their lot with the Covenanters, and shared their sufferings in prison, on the scaffold, or by having ruinous fines levied on them.

The Laird of Carleton and Killochan took the side of the people. He is not so well known as the Laird who flourished in the beginning of that century, Sir John Cathcart, and who was famous in his day as a man of extraordinary piety. Although the Covenanting Laird does not figure in the history of the times, he went the length, at great risk to himself, of throwing open his dining hall to his tenantry and neighbours around for services, conducted by the outed Presbyterian ministers, at which the Lord's Supper was sometimes dispensed. How he managed to escape, whether by influence at head-quarters, or in some other way, we cannot tell.

The "Hall" in which the meetings were held is un-doubtedly the present dining-room, a large and spacious wainscotted room with family portraits of centuries of Cathcarts looking down grimly from the walls, and with wild boars' heads and other hunting trophies of the present respected proprietor, Sir Reginald Cathcart.

There were doubtless other Conventicles held in the hall, but the only one of which we have any record is that at which the Rev. Thomas Kennedy, of Lasswade, was present and preached. The Laird was there with his family and servants, and the room was well filled with a grave and reverent congregation. After the homely singing of a Psalm, and a fervent prayer, the preacher amid the hush of expectancy gave out as his text Psalm cxxix., dwelling much on the sufferings of the persecuted Church of Scotland on whose back, in the language of the Psalm, "the ploughers had ploughed making long their furrows." As he went on he became more pointed and personal, and pressed on his hearers the necessity and the blessedness of making choice of the Lord Jesus Christ as their Saviour, and casting in their lot, come weal or come woe, with Him and His people.

The sermon was very impressive, and seems to have been greatly blessed. We know of four young persons—doubtless there were more—who could trace their first religious impressions to that sermon. These were John Stevenson, the young farmer from Camregan, his sister, a young man named M'Connel, and his sister, Isabel, who afterwards became John Stevenson's wife and shared his sufferings.

CRAIGDOW CONVENTICLE.

Have any of our readers ever been on the top of Craigdow? It would be worth their while to visit it and try to recall the scene, so memorable in John Stevenson's experience, on that autumn afternoon nearly 200 years ago. Passing Newlands Farm, and ascending through a belting of wood, we soon find ourselves on the open, breezy, heathery moorland. At a point where the old cart road along which we are travelling appears to have been joined by an older road, now overgrown with grass and heather, stands a memorial of one of those " old, unhappy, far-off things" the poet speaks of, in the shape of a cairn of stones, marking the spot where, in consequence of a private feud, the Laird of Drummochreen was slain by Kennedy of Girvan Mains. We are now at the foot of the hill of Craigdow, and we here pass into Kirkoswald Parish—the stone fence running across the hill being the march. Were we to follow this road a little further, in a few minutes we should come in sight of the farm of Lochspouts, near which, amid picturesque surroundings, is another scene of interest, where we have a strange blending of extreme antiquity with present-day life. There is the new reservoir constructed for supplying Maybole with water, and it occupies the site of an ancient lake, which could never have been anything but of small dimensions. A few yards from what was the shore of that lake was discovered an ancient lake-dwelling or "Crannog," which, on excavation, yielded an interesting find of bones of animals, shells, bronze ornaments, and a variety of stone implements used by our savage Carrick progenitors in the prehistoric age.

Craigdow is a Celtic name, and, like other Celtic names, is expressive. It means "The Black Rock," and was so called from the jutting points of trap which diversify its slopes of grass and heather, as well as from the dark hues of the latter with which it is plentifully clothed. There are two summits, with a hollow between—that to the west presenting the greatest expanse; and it was here, probably it may have been in one of these grassy hollows, well suited to the purpose, where there would be some shelter from the wind, and comparative concealment, that the "Conventicle" was held. The view from the summit is extensive and varied, embracing Shalloch-on-Minnoch and the Highlands of Ayrshire to the east, and the blue Firth, the jagged ridges of Arran, the long Kintyre peninsula beyond, and Ailsa Rock conspicuous in the foreground, on the west. But it is not for the sake of the prospect, enhanced as it is by the purple bloom of the heather and the rich tints of autumn on the fields away yonder towards the north, that these groups of men, women, and children, in hodden grey, from far and near, are seen wending their way up the slopes of Craigdow—fisher folk from the shore over yonder, shepherds from the hills, farmers and farm labourers from the straths, with a sprinkling from the Castle and mansion-house. They are there at a dreadful risk to feed upon the Word of God from the lips of one of their beloved ministers, who are outed and persecuted, John Welsh of Kirkpatrick - Irongray, Dumfriesshire, for the news has been secretly circulated from mouth to mouth throughout Carrick that he is to preach that day on the Hill of Craigdow. And now the watchmen have been posted to give warning of the approach of the troopers, and their figures may be seen against the sky on Kildoon Hill, Kirkhill, and other heights around. The opening Psalm is sung with heart and soul, and there are few voices that fail to swell the volume of plaintive melody, which is carried far on the breeze. The prayer which follows is a fervent wrestling with heaven for a blessing. Then the preacher, amid the hush of expectation, gives out as his text 2 Cor. v. 20—"We beseech you, be ye reconciled to God," and preaches a very earnest and impressive sermon. Tears may be seen trickling down many a cheek, and we know of one at least—probably there were more—who under that sermon was led to close with "Glorious Christ" and enter into the peace and joy of believing. Judging from the specimens we have of the hill preachings in those days, they seem to have been very solemn and stirring, and by no means confined to the subject of the sufferings and contendings of the times. They were full of rousing Gospel appeals and warnings, with the view of leading the soul to a personal and earnest decision for Christ.

F

CHAPTER VI.

THE PARISH CHURCH.

OLD DAILLY CHURCH.

WE cannot say for certain whether the present roofless ruin is the remains of the identical church which was gifted with its revenues by the First Earl of Carrick to the Monastery of Paisley, and afterwards transferred by King Robert the Bruce to Crossraguel, but if there was a still older church, it would probably occupy the same site. The present ruin is undoubtedly very ancient, and was used as a church long before the Reformation. An antiquarian friend gives it as his opinion, judging from its form and the style of its architecture, that it cannot be of later date than the 14th century, and that possibly it may be much earlier. It is beautifully situated about three miles to the east of Girvan, at a point where the hill country sinks into the vale, and where the brawling Penquhapple burn emerges from its wooded glen and now ripples gently along towards the Girvan, which it joins a few hundred yards down the valley, near where once stood the old farm-steading of Dalquhir. At a short distance to the north of the church stand the gables of the old manse, the side walls having been

82

removed to make way for the plough. The old church, partially covered with ivy and shaded by old trees, one of which has entwined its roots into the north wall, on the spot where the pulpit used to stand, the surrounding graveyard where seven centuries of the dead repose—a link connecting us with the days of the Crusaders and King Robert the Bruce—the graves of martyred Covenanters, the many old stones, some of them unlettered save by the finger of time, the numerous "mouldering heaps" over the nameless dead, the whole scene being reverently guarded and secluded from the world by ancient trees, all this makes even the careless and unimaginative feel that here "the place whereon they stand is holy ground."

Like all ancient churches, the building stands due east and west. In length it is about 92 feet, in breadth 25 feet, over the walls. Each of the two gables is surmounted by a belfry. A cross formerly stood on the eastern belfry, but it was knocked down by the branch of a tree during a storm about a century ago. The double belfry is a very unusual circumstance, and testifies to the ancient importance of our old church. The western bell was used in Roman Catholic times for summoning the people to worship, while the eastern or "sanctus bell" was only rung when the more solemn services of the Church were being performed. The "Piscina," a stone basin in which the priests washed their hands and also rinsed the chalice at the celebration of the mass, is said still to remain in the wall, within the tomb of the Bargany family, in the east end of the building. The pulpit, since the Reformation, seems to have been placed near the middle of the north wall, and, considering the length and narrowness of the building, this was no doubt the most suitable arrangement. The north wall is partly broken down, but access to the pulpit appears to have been obtained by a doorway through the wall. The tree which grows on the wall where the pulpit stood is said to be the fulfilment of a prophecy by Alexander Peden, the Covenanter, of whom there are various local traditions. The south wall is entire, and is remarkable for two doors, the one being arched and wide, while the other, which was probably a private entrance, is low and narrow. On this side of the building there is only one small window, and to all appearance, unless it was lighted from the roof, the worshippers would be largely favoured with "the dim religious light."

THE PRESENT PARISH CHURCH.

Public worship was discontinued at Old Dailly and a new church was built at Milcavish, afterwards called New Dailly, in 1690. Close by the new church there was a manse built. We have no record of what the church was like, but it was a credit neither to the heritors nor to the tradesmen of the day, as it had become decayed only about seventy years after it was erected. The manse also appears to have been badly constructed, for about five years before the church was taken down, in 1758, a new manse, the present one, was built at a cost of £190, on what is now the glebe, but where in Pont's time, in the early part of the 17th century, stood the farm of "Polmachow," at the junction of "Polmachow burn" with the Girvan.

In 1763 steps were taken by the minister, the Rev. Thomas Thomson, to get the church rebuilt. He arranged a meeting of the Presbytery with the heritors, and got tradesmen appointed to inspect and report on the state of the church. The inspection took place on 28th April, 1763, and the following is the report :—

"We, ye undersubscribers, being appointed by the Heritors and Presbytery to visit and inspect ye condition of ye Kirk of Dailly, did accordingly inspect ye said Kirk, and we give it as our opinion unanimously yt it is altogether in a bad state and cannot be repaired, which we are willing to make faith upon if required. Sic subscributur Alex. M'Keirly, mason (Maybole); Peter Dickson, wright; Robert Thomson, wright (at Killochan); Wm. Smith, mason (Old Dailly); John Galt, mason; Charles Campbell, slater."

The Presbytery's deliverance is as follows :—"Upon which report ye Presbytery did, and hereby do, declare ye present Kirk of Dailly insufficient, and yt it is necessary to build a new one."

An old man, who died a good many years ago, used to tell that he was present and assisted at the taking down of the old church. It appears that the minister, a stout, ponderous man, lent a helping hand, and as he was pulling away with a will at a rope attached to one of the gables, the wall gave way quicker than was expected, and the whole party of pullers fell down in a heap, the man from whom our information comes, and who was immediately behind the minister, being left struggling, partly smothered and partly bruised by the weighty "body of divinity" which fell upon him.

The new church was finished in 1766, and cost £600. Although of no great architectural beauty, it is a more substantial structure than its predecessor appears to have been. The heritors, however, fell into the mistake of making it too small for the population of the parish, as it was found necessary, twelve years after it was built, that is, in 1778, to make a considerable addition by the building of "the aisle," giving an increase of about 100 sittings, making in all 600 sittings.

CHAPTER VII.

GLIMPSES OF THE PAST FROM KIRK-SESSION MINUTES.

THE KIRK-SESSION MINUTES.

THE old Session records of the parishes of Scotland which have survived are often dreary, and sometimes painful, reading, but they are very valuable for the light which they shed upon the old church life and the general manners and customs of the times.

Our records are far from complete. The oldest dates from 1691. They go on continuously from that date to 1702. Then from 1702 to 1711 there is a blank. There are continuous records from 1711 to 1759. Then occurs a blank extending over 40 years. Thereafter they are unbroken. In many parishes the old records are still scantier. In some they have altogether disappeared. Left in the custody, perhaps, of the Session Clerks, at their death they might pass into the hands of some who did not know the value of them, and with no one sufficiently interested to make inquiry after them, and with, perhaps, lax supervision by Presbyteries over them, we can easily understand how volumes of the records would get lost. It is said that it was found when too late that a large portion

87

of the oldest records of the Parish of Barr had been used for kindling fires.

CHURCH CENSURES.

Two hundred years ago the Kirk-Session was what might be called the "Local Authority" of the parish. It had great power, and the parishioners stood greatly in awe of it. Breaches of the seventh commandment were by far the most common offences that came under its jurisdiction. Hence the minutes of the Kirk-Session away back in those early times are not all edifying reading. But in addition the Kirk-Session took cognisance of other acts, such as drinking on the Sabbath, other breaches of the Sabbath, such as gathering nuts, mending fences, or doing other unnecessary work, breaches of the Fast Day, as well as of the Sabbath, absence from public worship, railing, scolding, etc. The punishment to which culprits were subjected was "public rebuke," that is, rebuke in presence of the congregation. In the case of minor offences the rebuke was sometimes only in the presence of the Kirk-Session. Sometimes a fine was exacted, the proceeds going to the fund in the Session's hands for the benefit of the poor. The place where delinquents had to stand when undergoing rebuke was called the "place of repentance," or the "repentance *stool*." But the word stool is misleading to a modern reader. In old times it had a wider meaning than now. The repentance stool was a *pillar* of moderate height, and is often called by that name, on which the parties stood "heich" in full view of the congregation.

Sometimes the culprit was allowed to stand "laich."
Sometimes it was considered sufficient that he should stand
up in his own seat. We have heard that this was done in
Dr. Hill's time, when public rebukes in this parish finally
disappeared. In the records there is mention made of
sackcloth, a garment of coarse linen, which had to be put on
when the offence was grave. Sometimes accused persons
had to find caution for compearance before the Session.
There is one instance of the Session ordering the apprehension of a fugitive from discipline. Sometimes parties
had to find security or subscribe "bonds" in pledge of
their good conduct in future. There is no mention in any
of our records of "the jougs." These were dying out by
the time our records begin. They were iron collars put
round the neck of delinquents, and used to form part of the
furniture of every church. They were attached to a pillar
in front of the church, or to the wall of the church itself,
and are still to be seen in some old churches, such as
Fenwick. It was only in extreme cases that Sessions had
recourse to the "jougs."

The following is an extract from one of our earliest
records :—

"December 19th, 1692, Margaret Ferguson compeared
and confessed that there was drinking in her house on the
Sabbath day, was rebuked, upon her promise not to suffer
the like again was dismissed." A few weeks after John
Houston, who was probably one of Margaret's drouthy
customers, was hauled up. It appears that in the course
of the previous autumn one Sunday instead of going to

church John had taken a stroll up one of the glens. Somebody either saw him gathering hazel nuts, or supposed that this was his errand. When John came down and had got the length of Margaret's he felt a little thirsty, and could not resist the temptation to step in for a refresher, heedless of the fact that at that moment the Rev. Patrick Crawford was wrestling with his afternoon sermon. John was summoned and compeared. He stoutly denied the nut gathering, but pled guilty to the drinking, for which he was rebuked, and, "having promised that he would not do the like again, was dismissed."

Two hundred years ago there were two diets of worship in the church, as there continued to be till within living memory. During the interval the ale-house or change-house was largely taken advantage of by those who came from a distance. There is evidence in the records that some of the congregation preferred Meg Ferguson's ale to the afternoon sermon. Examples were made of some of them. They were rebuked by the Session, and made to promise that they would never do the like again. Meg herself got a rebuke for selling the drink. In 1711 an elder and a deacon were appointed by the Session to search the change-houses during the service, and probably to report any cases of persons they found there.

But there were other forms of Sabbath-breaking which Sessions in those days felt it their duty to deal with. For instance, there was a parishioner of the name of Robert Carson, who added to his ordinary handicraft that of a barber. One Sabbath day—it was in the summer of 1695

—he was called on by some men who wanted him to give them a shave. According to his own statement Robert at first refused. It was the Sabbath day; he had never done it, and what would the minister and elders say? The men threatened him, and he had to give in to superior force. No notice was taken of his offence at the time, but shortly after, as he and his family were leaving the parish, he applied to the minister for his and their " testificats." The request was refused on the ground that " it was informed against him that he was guilty of profaning the Sabbath by taking off beards," the Session appoint him to be " publickly rebuked and gett his testificat."

We have a few interesting sidelights in these old records on the social life and customs of the day. This is one— as far back as 1697 potatoes were grown in this parish. Here is another. In a case before the Session in 1694, in which evidence was led, there is a casual mention by one of the witnesses of the "goat bught" at Drumburl, from which we may gather that at that period goats, sometimes at least, formed part of a Dailly farmer's stock. Here is another. In the course of evidence in a case in 1733 mention is made of a woman's *snuff mill*. We know that it was a common thing for Scottish ladies of that period to take snuff. It appears from this reference that the custom extended to females of all ranks.

As an example of the power which Sessions took upon themselves without a word of complaint from the parishioners — in a case before them in November 1694, it was reported that James Thomson, who had been summoned before them, had fled to Ireland, and that as Jean

M'Clure, the partner of his guilt, designed to follow him, the minister and Drummelland are appointed to desire Lord Barganie to apprehend her. At the next meeting the minister reported that Lord Barganie had apprehended Jean "until she found caution not to leave the Parish for the period of ane year, and all that time to be subject to Church discipline, under the penalty of ane hundred pounds Scots."

THE COMMUNION AND "HOLY FAIRS."

The references to the Communion in the old records are not very frequent. The custom prevailed over the country up till well on in the last century of parishioners of neighbouring parishes flocking to one of the churches in the district for the Communion services, their own churches being shut up for the day. The ministers were present and took part. There was a long succession of tables, and the service went on from 10 o'clock in the morning till well on in the afternoon, sometimes late in the evening. Communion services have been known to last for twelve hours; and while the "tables" were being served inside the church by a succession of ministers, another succession held forth to a changing congregation from the "tent" in the churchyard. The tent was a movable pulpit made of wood for the preacher to stand in under cover, and open towards the congregation, seated in picturesque groups on the graves or on forms set out on the level ground. While the minister was preaching another was at hand, ready to take his place when he was done. All the time the ale-houses in the neighbourhood of the church were driving a roaring trade.

But the best things are abused, and these big gatherings were abused. All who have read Burns' "Holy Fair" know how. That poem rung their death-knell. But they continued, though not to the same extent, down to within living memory. Dailly was no exception to the above state of matters. There are local traditions of drinking to excess and fighting on these occasions. Dr. Hill, who became minister of the parish in 1816, was keenly alive to the evils which had grown around these Communions, and induced his Kirk-Session to discontinue them. This was the first parish in the district where they were given up. They were continued in the neighbouring parishes for years after, but the evils were not abated, and these parishes were forced by public opinion to follow the example of Dailly, and "tent preachings" or "holy fairs" became things of the past.

We have only one or two very meagre references in the Session records to such occasions in this parish. Where these occur they give little more than the number of communicants and the number of officiating ministers. We must remember that over and above the communicants there were hundreds present who were not communicants. At the Dailly Communion in 1749, 549 persons communicated, of whom 293 belonged to the parish and 256 were strangers. Four ministers and a "preacher," probably a young probationer, assisted, the latter taking his turn in the tent. In May of the following year, 1750, there were distributed to communicants in the parish 300 "tickets," to strangers 340. On that occasion there were five ministers and a preacher. In the minute dated May of the following year there is a much fuller record. At the Communion in that month 711 " tickets" were given in. The congregation met at ten forenoon, and the service continued till twenty minutes past two. The tickets or tokens were square bits of lead manufactured and stamped by Kirk-Sessions themselves. Many of the Dailly tokens are still in existence. They are very plain, having simply the name of the parish stamped on them thus—$\frac{DA}{LY}$.

THE KIRK-SESSION AND POOR RELIEF.

We have seen that at the time to which we have referred, two hundred years ago, Kirk-Sessions were the supreme authority in parishes, and that they ruled with a rod of iron. It is easy for us to condemn the intolerance and harshness of their discipline, and the want of perspective shown, for example, in putting breaches of the Fast Day on a level with serious moral offences. At the same time we must not forget the good work which they did. They were a "terror to evil-doers." Gross crimes would have been far more common in these rude and comparatively lawless days but for the stool of repentance, the sackcloth, and the jougs. Then there was the relief of the poor of the parish, the burden of which they bore for three hundred years, and this is the strongest claim they have upon our gratitude. Down to 1845 there were no poor rates in Scotland, no Parochial Boards, no Inspectors of Poor. The money for the support of the poor was raised and distributed without cost to the parish by Kirk-Sessions. The money was raised chiefly by collections at the church door. In March, 1693, the Kirk-Session of Dailly appointed an extraordinary collection every month for the poor of the parish. In 1845 all this was changed. Partly owing to the increase of pauperism, and partly owing to the Disruption of 1843, which was such a serious blow to the Church and curtailed the power of Kirk-Sessions, it became necessary to make a legal provision for the support of the poor through the machinery of Parochial Boards and poor rates. But the old system, which brought the charity of the Church to bear on the relief of the poor so that it came "as a matter of bounty and not of necessity," was more in keeping with the spirit of Christianity and more beneficial both to giver and receiver. The divorce of the relief of the poor from Christian charity and making it a thing of legislation, of compulsory rate-paying and paid officialism may have been a necessity, but the old custom was more in keeping with the mind of Him who left the poor as a legacy to His Church. "The poor ye have always with you, but Me ye have not always."

We find the Kirk-Session appointing collections for other objects than the relief of the poor. On 23rd November, 1693, James M'Hutcheson of Blair, one of the elders, got a collection "to carry to Air for Andro King, slave with the Turks." At that time British sailors sometimes fell into the hands of pirates on the coast of Barbary or elsewhere, and were held captive till ransomed by their friends, and it was to help the fund for the redemption of Andrew that the Session appointed the collection to be made.

The parishes of Ayrshire in the last century seem to have been greatly infested with vagrants. In 1752 two Acts of the Justices of the Peace for the County were laid before the Kirk-Session. By these it was enacted that all vagrant persons should withdraw from the Shire within a certain date, under the penalty of being apprehended, incarcerated, and fed on bread and water for ten days, and also ordaining the poor of the Shire to repair to their respective parishes where they were born or have resided for the last three years, and make application to the Kirk-Session and heritors. The Session agreed to make up lists of the poor of this parish, who are to be served with "badges," and allowed to beg within the parish, "certifying them that if they be found begging in any other parish, their badges shall be taken from them, and that such as are capable of any work, if they shall neglect to work, though not able to maintain themselves by their work, the badge shall be taken from them."

In spite of the action of the civil and ecclesiastical authorities, vagrancy continued to prevail. In 1773 the Synod and Presbytery had to take action. In a Dailly Session minute of that year it is recorded that "the Presbytery recommend to all their members to read the Synod's Act against vagrant beggars, and also that no minister or elder shall give alms to any vagrant beggars, and that they use their influence, both public and private, with their parishioners that they do the same."

There is one object which comes well to the front in these ancient records, and that is "the Box." The box, which, as we find from an entry for repairs, was mounted with brass, contained the monies of the Session, on which the comfort and even the life of not a few of the parishioners depended. On a certain day once a year the Session held a special meeting to "visit" or "inspect" the box. At one inspection of the box it was found that the "base brass" represented the sum of no less than £2 9s. 5d. In 1748 the experts of the Session discovered among the base brass a bad shilling, which they at once, doubtless in presence of the Session, caused to be "destroyed." As we cannot suppose that all this bad money was put into the collection by mistake, this is surely an indication of a very low tone of morality—not to speak of religion.

But the box was not altogether dependent on the church door collections. These were comparatively small; they were sometimes little over one shilling, and very seldom above eight. And there were frequent vacant Sundays. But the Session had other sources of revenue. There was the interest on mortifications, sums bequeathed to them by parishioners for the benefit of the poor. Then there were the small penalties inflicted in cases of discipline, "marriage bills," which we call "proclamation dues," collections, ranging from one shilling upwards, levied at marriages, and mortcloth dues. Besides, the heritors not only contributed when present at church; some of them sent contributions annually or on the occasion of marriages or deaths in the family. For instance, Sir Adam Fergusson, on the occasion of the death and burial in the churchyard of his father, Lord Kilkerran, gave the Session five pounds to be distributed among the poor of the parish. The Lairds of

Bargany and Dalquharran are repeatedly mentioned as
sending their "complement" of £1—*e.g.*, "Oct. 25, 1747,
by Baron Kennedy's complement, £1 ; by Mr. Kennedy of
Dalquharran's marriage, 10s. 6d."

The Kirk-Session moreover tried to increase their
revenue by doing a little financing. Some of the lairds
did not think it beneath them to do business with the box.
On one occasion, it was in 1748, the Laird of Penkill,
Alexander Boyd, had a "transaction" with the Session.
He was not long away till he returned with a gold
coin in his hand which he said he had got from them
as a *half-guinea*, but which was only a "quarter Johannis,"
the Johannis being a Portuguese coin worth 36 shillings.
It was called a "Joe." The laird had only got a "quarter
Joe." As the Session reimbursed him with three shillings
he must have got two quarter Joes instead of two half-
guineas, eighteen shillings instead of twenty-one shillings.
One of the deacons, for there were deacons in these
days, was a shoemaker and lived at "Waulkmill." In one
reference to him he is said to live at "Fordhouse." His
name was John M'Clellan. John did not see why he
should not get the benefit of the Session's financing, so
he borrowed £2 2s. 5d., and paid it back to the last
penny in boots and shoes for the poor.

The money aliment was distributed weekly in sums
ranging from 6d. to 2s., but the latter sum was rare. One
shilling was a very common allowance. The Session also
made grants of articles of clothing, sometimes paying
the tradesmen, sometimes giving material. It is interesting
to note the prices. Blankets ranged from 1s. 3d. to

4s., women's shoes from 1s. to 2s., men's from 2s. 6d. to 3s. 2d. Janet Stewart got half a stone of wool to spin and weave. It cost the Session 3s. 6d. Here is another entry in 1746—"To cloth and making John M'Callan's breeches, 1s. 6d."

The Session acted sometimes on the good principle of helping people to help themselves. For instance, in June, 1750, they gave James Kennedy 1s. 9d. " for relief of the *linnen work*," or flax work, at one or other of the waulk mills with which James had somehow got into difficulties. In the same year James Kennedy of Carscull got 7s. 6d. from the box to help to pay for a horse, and in 1756 James M'Candlish, "coal cadger," got the same sum for the same object, and so he was able to keep his cart going to and from the "coal heugh." Sometimes the box also helped people to build houses for themselves, for almost anybody in these days could build a house that was considered good enough to live in. In the early summer of 1751 a man whose name occurs frequently in the poor lists, Nicolas or Nicky M'Candlish, thought he would like to have a house of his own. The Session came to his help with 5s. When his house was at length finished Nicky was no doubt proud of it. "It was wee, but it was his ain." In October, 1758, Nicky had to leave for a still narrower house, and here again the kindly Session came to his help with the same sum. Here is an entry on October 29th of that year—"To Nicky M'Candlish's coffin, 5s."

THE CARRICK CLASS.

Church life, like all other life, was quieter and slower in the olden time than now. There were few schemes, organisations, or public meetings of any kind. Still we find the existence within this Presbytery and elsewhere of an institution which had a similiar object in view as our conference. It was not, however, called by that name. It was called a " classis."

It is a Latin word, a word which usually means *fleet*, though it had another meaning which survives in our word *class*.

In Holland, after the Reformation, which in that country, as well as in ours, took the Presbyterian form, the word *classis* came to be applied to a stated meeting of pastors and ruling elders of churches nearly neighbouring, chiefly for the exercise of discipline in their churches. In other words, it was practically what we call a Presbytery.

But in the Presbytery of Ayr, *classis*, or class, was used in a different sense. The class was not composed of the whole Presbytery, but of a part which met statedly for prayer and the discussion of questions of common interest, theological or other. In a minute of Presbytery of date 1697 we read that "the several 'classes' that meet sometimes for prayer are appointed to meet those of Carrick at Daillie and those of Kyle at Symington, St. Quivox and Auchinleck." Another minute of date 1737 states that in the Presbytery there were four classes, those of Cumnock, Galston, Ayr, and Maybole. We have been told by the late Dr. Chrystal, of Auchinleck, who was ordained to that parish in 1833, that at that time and for some years after, the Carrick class was in the habit of holding its meetings in Dailly Manse, an essay or paper being read by one of the members and remarks made upon it or the subject by others. The well-known Dr. M'Knight, of Maybole, who was Moderator of the General Assembly in 1766 and the author of a work on the New Testament entitled a "Harmony of the Four Gospels," which a local wit called "Trying to mak' fowre men 'gree wha never cast oot," used to attend these meetings, and it is said that papers read by him at the "classical meeting" at Dailly formed the basis of this work. He was an able man but a dry preacher. One wet Sunday morning he arrived at the vestry "drookit." "John," he said to the beadle, "I'm all wet." "Never mind, doctor," said the beadle, "you'll be dry eneuch when ye get into the poopit."

The "classis," we may mention before leaving the subject, was sometimes appointed by the Presbytery of Ayr to take some action in cases of discipline, and with the addition sometimes of other members to visit grammar schools. In 1738 the Presbytery appointed the brethren of the Class of Ayr, along with other three members, to visit the Grammar School of Ayr, and the Classes of Cumnock, Maybole, and Galston are each appointed "to visit the grammar schools that are in each of their bounds at their first classical meeting."

CHAPTER VIII.

LAIRDS AND THEIR LANDS.

THE BOYDS OF PENKILL.

THE first recorded ancestor of the Boyds was Simon, brother of Walter, the first High Steward of Scotland. He died some time before 1240. Later on King Robert the Bruce granted certain lands to his gallant adherent, Sir Robert Boyd, the ancestor of the Earls of Kilmarnock. Later on in the same line there was a Robert Lord Boyd, who figures in history as Chamberlain of Scotland, during the minority of James III. From him the Boyds of Penkill and Trochrague are descended. The last of the Earls of Kilmarnock took part in the "Forty-five" and was afterwards executed for high treason and the title declared forfeited.

The first of the Boyds who rose to fame was

MARK ALEXANDER BOYD.

He was son of Robert Boyd of Penkill, and grandson of the Chamberlain. He was born in 1562. He was educated with his uncle James, "Tulchan," Archbishop of

102

Glasgow. Violent in temper, he quarrelled with his teachers, gave up his studies, and latterly, from the same cause, he had to retire from Scotland and seek refuge in France. After a wandering, restless life, partly taken up with the study of civil law, he joined the Roman Catholic party, although a Protestant, in the wars of the League. On the conclusion of the campaign in 1588, he resumed his legal studies, between which and soldiering he continued to live an unsettled life, finding time, however, to publish certain poetical effusions in Latin, the language of the learned in those days. He is said to have been able to dictate at once in three different languages to three amanuenses. He died at Penkill in 1601 in the fortieth year of his age. Next on the roll of fame of the Boyds stands the name of

ROBERT BOYD OF TROCHRIG,

son of James Boyd, the Archbishop, and cousin of the above. He was born at Glasgow in 1578. Studying at Edinburgh, and afterwards in France, he made great proficiency, particularly in Greek, Latin, and Hebrew. He became a professor of philosophy at Montauban in France, and afterwards at Saumur. He was also a minister of the French Reformed Church. The fame of his learning reaching his native country, James the First of England sent for him, and appointed him professor of divinity and Principal of the University of Glasgow. In connection with this appointment he held the charge of Govan. His lectures were delivered in Latin, but with as much freedom as if they had been spoken in his native tongue. Principal

Baillie, who studied under him, mentions the deep impression made upon the students by the fervour of his Latin prayers. Refusing to sign the five "Articles of Perth" by which the King tried to assimilate the Presbyterian to the Episcopal form of Church Government, he retired to Trochrig, but was afterwards elected Principal of the University of Edinburgh, very much to the annoyance of the King. In consequence of the royal remonstrance with the Provost, Bailies, and Council, he retired to his estate. He was subsequently minister of Paisley, and died at Edinburgh, or, as some say, at Trochrig, in 1627, aged forty-eight.

But the best known name among the Boyds is that of

ZACHARY BOYD,

cousin of the above. He also studied in France, where for a time he attended his cousin's classes in the University of Saumur, where he afterwards became a professor himself. On account of the persecution of the Protestants he came home, and in 1623 was appointed minister of the Barony Parish, Glasgow, where he continued till his death. Three times over he was elected Rector of the University of Glasgow. He signed the solemn League and Covenant. When Cromwell came to Glasgow he "railed" on him and his soldiers to their face from the pulpit of the Barony so that one of the officers wanted to "pistol the scoundrel." "No," said Cromwell, "we will manage him another way." He invited him to dinner, and by the length and fervour of his devotions so won the respect of Zachary that he had not another word to say against him. He died in 1653 or

the beginning of 1654, and was succeeded by Donald
Cargill, one of the martyrs of the Covenant. He was in
harness to the last. Shortly before he died he finished a
work entitled: "The Notable Places of the Scriptures
Expounded," at the conclusion of which he added: "Heere
the author was neere his end, and was able to do no more."
It is said that when he was making his will his wife—one
of the Renfrewshire Mures—requested him to leave something to Mr. Durham, a minister, and a great favourite with
both. "No, no, Margaret," was his reply, "I'll lea' him
naething but thy bonnie sel'." Another version is: "I'll
lea' him what I canna' keep frae him." Mrs. Boyd afterwards became Mrs. James Durham. His property, which
was considerable, was divided between her and the
University of Glasgow. His bust, with an inscription
commemorating his various benefactions, stood over the
entrance to the second quadrangle of the Old University
Buildings in the High Street. He left behind him many
works, the best known of which are a metre version of the
Psalms—which competed with our version (by Rous) for its
place in the Psalmody of the Church of Scotland—"The
last Battell of the Soull in Death," and "Zion's Flowers,"
or "Christian Poems for Spiritual Edification," which con-
sist of verses on select subjects in scripture history, very
quaint, homely, and even ludicrous sometimes, but with a
fine strain of devotional feeling running through them.

DALQUHARRAN OLD CASTLE.

There is a still older ruin of the same name in Lochmoddy glen, overhanging Lochmoddy burn, and quite close upon the railway, which has greatly spoiled the natural beauty of the spot. There is a tradition that the building was never completed, the Prince of Darkness, for some reason or other, having taken umbrage at its erection and pulled down during the night what was built during the day. But there can be no doubt the castle was completed and inhabited. It must have been much more extensive than is indicated by the existing remains. It is said that the stones were largely used in building the new, which is now called the old castle, and this may account for the smallness of the ruin. And the discovery in the present old castle of stones bearing marks of an older date than its erection confirms this idea.

The age of this older castle is unknown. But we find from the Glasgow Commissary Records that there was a residence at "Dalquhuran" as early as the year 1536. In that year, and at Dalquhuran, "Johnn Kennedy of Culzeane signed an obligation binding himself to resign the superiority of the lands of Drummellane to Patrick Kennedy of Balmaclanachan."

If stones were taken from it to build the new house, a sufficient portion was left to be habitable. We find from the Kirk-Session records that a certain witness in a case before the Session is called "the wife of Thomas M'Lewrath, residing in the old castle of Dalquharran." That was in

the year 1722, or 45 years after the building of the castle
on the bank of the Girvan.

To pass to the old castle which now goes by that name,
we find that there are two dates on it indicating that it was
begun in 1677 and added to in 1679. The former date is
over a window in the interior of the second story, along
with the initials S.I.K., D.M.K., the same initials being
carved on the mantelpiece of what appears to have been
the drawing-room (in those days called the "withdrawing"
room), on the same story. The date 1679 is over the
principal doorway, and underneath is a line of Latin verse
in the style of the monkish rhymes handed down from the
middle ages:

"Ut Scriptura sonat finis non pugna coronat."

which may be translated—

"'Tis not the fight, so Scripture cries,
It is the end that gives the prize."

The reference seems to be to Paul's saying—"I have fought
the good fight, I have finished my course, I have kept the
faith, henceforth there is laid up for me a crown of
righteousness." There are few sweeter spots in our parish
than the old garden, now partially cleared of trees and
re-arranged, stretching away in velvety lawn, variegated with
shrubs and flowers, down to the old, gray, ivy-mantled
walls and turrets, the haunt of the owl, and lively with the
chattering of jackdaws, the scene to the south in the
direction of the river being bounded by the "crow wood,"
with magnificent Scotch firs, in whose top branches a noisy
colony of rooks has been settled from time immemorial.

We are able to give our readers a glimpse of the castle
and its surroundings as they existed nearly 200 years ago,
and not long after the castle was built. During the reign
of Episcopacy there was an Episcopalian clergyman in the
Parish of Maybole (then spelt "Minnibole") named
William Abercrummie. He superseded John Hutcheson,
the Presbyterian minister there, but was himself ousted by
Hutcheson's return at the Revolution. Abercrummie, who
seems to have been of an observant nature, wrote a history
of Carrick which is extant. As he refers to the removal of
the Parish Church from Old Dailly to New Dailly as a
recent event, the time at which he writes must be near the
end of the 17th century. He follows the course of
the river in his description of our district. After a glowing
picture of "the House of Drummochren" he says—"Not
far from this, downe the water, stands the stately castle of
Dolquharran, the building whereof is much improved by
additions lately made thereto (the addition of 1679, or
something later), which make it by very far the best house
of all that country, surrounded by vast enclosures of wood,
that the country is not able to consume it by their building
and other instruments. And amongst them there be oak
trees of a considerable size, that will serve either for jest
(joist) or roofe of good houses." There are still a number
of very fine oaks in the Dalquharran grounds, more
especially in the neighbourhood of Dowhail, some of which
were no doubt in existence in the historian's day.

KILKERRAN OLD CASTLE.

The Castle of Kilkerran was built on a plateau extending to the edge of the wooded ravine through which the Kilkerran or Lindsayston burn flows. It was evidently designed to be a place of strength, and speaks of the troublous times of war or foray. At the same time there are indications of more settled and peaceful days in the remains of a terraced walk overhanging the stream, and partly cut out of the face of the curious " puddingstone " or " conglomerate " rock, which at one part also bears traces of a grotto with seats formed out of the rock. Below there is a small waterfall, the burn here taking two leaps, the second of which, where it plunges itself into a deep, dark pool, forms with its rocky and leafy surroundings a very pretty picture.

A short distance above the fall the main stream receives two affluents, the Delamford burn and the Dobbingstone burn. In far back times there was a house with lands called " Burnfute " occupied as far back as 1508 by a young heir of Kilkerran before coming to his inheritance. It is probable that it stood at this point somewhere near the meeting of the waters, hence the name.

The following is the reference in the ancient records. It is quoted in " Paterson's History of Ayrshire " from the " Books of Adjournal." It gives us a lurid glimpse into the social condition of the parish 380 years ago. In the above year " John Schaw of Kerise was admitted to compound for art and part of the forethought ffelony done to

Duncan Fergussoune, young laird of Kilkerane, in coming
to his place of Burnefute and throwing down and breaking
into the houses of the said place, and for forcibly keeping
the lands of Burnefute waste for the space of one year."

In the beginning of last century the ruins of Kilkerran
Castle were almost entire. Since then it has been greatly
encroached upon by time, and probably also by the hand
of man. The last serious calamity to it happened about
1870. One day, just a day or two after an inspection had
been made of the building, which had been showing signs
of giving way, to see if anything could be done to preserve
it, a large portion came down in sight of two of the
neighbours with a thunderous crash and amid clouds of
dust, falling in immense solid blocks, showing the strength
and substantial character of the ancient masonry. All that
is left standing now is the lofty gable, with its corbie steps
and a portion of two side walls attached, the floor supported
by a massive arch covering what appears to have been
the ancient kitchen. Still there is enough left standing to
give us some idea of the grandeur of the original structure.

We do not know when the castle was built. Some think
from its architecture it may be as old as the 13th or 14th
century. But whether the present castle was built then or
not it is probable that there was a house here in the days
of King Robert the Bruce. The family of the Fergussons
of Kilkerran first come into notice in his day, and the
residence of the family was always here till about 200 years
ago.

King Robert the Bruce, doubtless for military services,
made a grant of certain lands in Ayrshire to " Fergus, son

of Fergus." The next glimpse we get into the history of the family in those early times is in 1466, when John Fergusson resigns a portion of his estate which is confirmed by charter under the hand of James III. to Fergus Fergusson his son and Janet Kennedy his spouse.

During the civil wars the family sustained a serious reverse of fortune. The then representative, Sir John Fergusson, was a staunch Royalist, and his attachment to the Royal cause led him to impoverish himself and incur a heavy debt, the only reward he received from the King being the honour of knighthood. His estates were sequestrated by Oliver Cromwell and fell into the hands of his neighbour, the Lord Bargany.

Sir John's youngest son was Simon of Auchinwinn. Simon again had a son John, who, having studied for the Scottish bar, gained a name and fame as an advocate, and amassed considerable wealth. He advanced money to clear off the debt on the property, and in this way acquired the estate from the elder branches of the family. This was in 1700. He was created a baronet by Queen Anne in 1703.

It was in his time that the castle ceased to be the residence of the family and the oldest portion of the present Kilkerran house was built.

The site of the present house had been occupied for many generations by an old house or "tower" called Barclanachan, or Balmaclanachan. It was the residence of a very old family, a branch of the Kennedies of "the Cove," the ancient name of Culzean. As far back as 1361, in the 32nd year of King David's reign, John Kennedy

had a charter of confirmation of the lands of Balmaclanachan granted by the King, at "Dumbriton"
(Dumbarton).

It seems to have been towards the end of the 17th
century that the estates passed from the Kennedies into
the hands of their neighbours the Fergussons, as one of the
elder branches of the latter family, who was a party to the
above transaction by which Sir John became possessor of
the Kilkerran estate, is styled "John of Barclanachan."
Sir John himself had sat in the Scots parliament under the
same title, but when he entered into the estate he changed
the name to Kilkerran. The old house was still standing
when Abercrummie wrote his account of the district 200
years ago. He says, "Upon the South Syde, and at some
distance from the river, stands the House of Barclanachan
with its gardens and orchards, all which are surrounded by
a wood, all the water from this downward till near Daillie
being so covered with wood that it looks like a forrest." It
appears from the Session records of date 3rd May, 1696,
that there was an "old lady Barclonnoquhan" then living
and that she had a seat in the church. The last of the
race of which we have any record is Robert Kennedy of
Balmaclanachan, who was alive in 1722.

Sir John Fergusson, who restored the fortunes of his
house, was succeeded by his son, Sir James. Like his
father he devoted himself to the Bar, and eventually rose
to the Bench under the title of Lord Kilkerran. He
married Lady Jane Maitland. She was the only child of
Lord Maitland, son of the Earl of Lauderdale, and of Lady
Maitland, daughter of the Earl and Countess of Sutherland.

Kilkerran Old Castle

Dailly Parish Church
Photograph by A. Ritchie

This Lady Maitland, who seems to have been early left a widow, resided with her daughter at Kilkerran for about 20 years, and died at Edinburgh in 1747.

Sir James, Lord Kilkerran, died in 1759. He is believed to have been buried somewhere within the walls of the old castle.

It is probable that there was a burying-place of "consecrated" ground beside the chapel of Machrykill, about three-quarters of a mile to the north-west of the old castle, and that it is here where many of the older generations of the Fergussons and their people were laid to rest, though there are now no traces of tombstones or graves.

WHY DOES AILSA CRAIG BELONG TO THE PARISH OF DAILLY?

We have all heard the supernatural explanation of the witch who was flying through the air, carrying in her apron the rock which she had taken out of what is now Penwhapple Glen, to Ireland, when her apron string broke, and with the exclamation "What ails 'ee?" she let her burden fall into the sea, hence the name. To pass from fable to fact, in former times Ailsa formed part of the Barony of Knockgerran. For a time it was in the hands of the Monks of Crossraguel, but latterly fell back into the possession of the Earls of Cassillis, to whom it formerly belonged. In 1806, the then Earl of Cassillis was created Baron Ailsa, and in 1831 he was raised to the

H

still higher dignity of Marquess of Ailsa. Hence when the
Barony of Knockgerran changed hands, and came into the
possession of Mr. Mackie, the father of the late proprietor,
the island was retained by the Marquess on account of the
title.

But that does not wholly explain the connection of the
island rock with our parish. The true explanation we
believe to be this :—When parishes were originally formed,
which was about the 12th century, they were much
larger than they are now. For various reasons, such as
the division of the original estate, or the inconvenient
situation of the Parish Church, many parishes were sub-
divided and new parishes formed. Dalmakerran seems to
have been one of the original parishes, and extended to
the sea, including Ailsa Craig. The fact that churches
were built in situations central for the population of the
parish, and that our old Parish Church is situated only
one mile from the western boundary of the parish, and six
miles from the eastern, is a strong evidence that our parish
at one time extended much further to the west. It is
undeniable that it extended to the south and included
what is now the Parish of Barr, which was disjoined in
1653. As a further evidence that Dalmakerran originally
extended to the sea, we find an entry in the books of the
Glasgow Commissary Court of date 1639 in which
Girvan Mains is said to be in the "parochin of Daillie."
The change must have taken place centuries before; but
the writer may have been quoting from an old document
anterior to the sub-division, of which perhaps he was not
aware. There is confirmatory evidence, too, in the import-

ance attached to Dailly in the old time. It seems to have been one of those churches which in Roman Catholic times possessed the right of sanctuary, and tradition associates the famous blue stones with that right. Then again there is a belfry in each of the gables of the old church, which is somewhat rare in our old parish churches, the western bell being used for summoning the people to worship, while the eastern, or " Sanctus bell," was only employed when the more solemn services of the church were being performed. And further, as indicating the ancient importance of the church and parish, it appears from the register of ministers and readers for the year 1574, which was shortly after the Reformation, that " Dalie " was at that time supplied with a minister and also a reader, while Girvan and Kirkoswald had only readers. On account of the difficulty of getting ministers for the parishes at that time, three-fourths of the parishes were supplied with readers who were under the superintendence of the minister settled in the district. It must have been at a very early period, indeed, that Girvan was disjoined from Dailly, as we read of a vicar of Girvan swearing fealty to Edward I., and that was in 1296. Our theory, then, and we think it is well supported, is that the original Parish of Dailly or Dalmakerran extended to the sea, and included Ailsa Craig, and that when Girvan was constituted into a separate parish it was not considered expedient to make any change in regard to the Craig, on the ground that it belonged to the Barony of Knockgerran in the Parish of Dailly.

[For the Origin of Bargany, *see* chap. iv.]

CHAPTER IX.

THE VALLEY OF GIRVAN COAL FIELD.

EARLY CHARTERS.

COAL was wrought in Scotland, and was a source of wealth as far back as the 13th century. Confining our view to the Water of Girvan Coal Field, the earliest record of the industry takes us back to the year 1415. Among the records of the Abbey of Crossraguel there has survived a charter of that date. It is by John M'Gillelane, "Lord of the half of the Over Barony of Glenstyncher commonly called Dalcharne (Dalquhairn)," then, like the rest of what is now the Parish of Barr, in the Parish of Dailly. It is in favour of his "very dear friend" Fergus Kennedy, Lord of Bonumyn, otherwise called *Buckmonyn*, in the Earldom of Lennox. The name now takes the form of *Buchanan*, and designates a parish in the shire of Dumbarton, the ancient Lennox country. It appears that in the year 1290 for services rendered, the Earl of Lennox had granted that estate to Gilbert de Carrick, and Fergus Kennedy had inherited it from him. In addition to his being a very dear friend of the Laird of Glenstyncher, Fergus had other claims upon him. He had helped him "in his great

necessity," and it was partly in repayment of money
advances that the Charter was drawn out. The Charter is
in the rude Latin in which these documents were expressed,
and in the description of the property transferred the
words occur — *Carbonariis lapide et calce* (coalpits stone
and limestone). And it is added that the property is to
be held of the Earl of Carrick, and the said Fergus is to
become bound "to do therefore the services due and
wont." Now as there is no coal, and never was any in
the valley of the Stinchar, the above clause can only be
explained by saying that the Over Barony of Glenstynchar
extended to that part of the Earldom of Carrick in our
valley, and included at least a portion of the coal field,
distant from the valley of Stinchar about five miles as the
crow flies. We are safe, then, in saying that we have
evidence of coal having been wrought in our valley nearly
500 years ago.

The next mention of coal in our district is in a Charter
of date 156-, the last figure not being legible. For
centuries the wealth of the great Abbey of Crossraguel had
been gradually accumulating. The greater part of Carrick
owed allegiance to it. But the Church was now in a
transition state. The Reformation was in process. The
first General Assembly of the Reformed Church had been
held (1560). The monks were in a state of alarm. The
Earl of Cassillis and other lairds were beginning to make
raids on the property of the Abbey. The former took the
Commendator of the Abbey, Alan Stewart, to his Black
Vault at Dunure, and held him before a slow fire till in
his extremity of torture he signed away some of the Abbey

lands. There are indications in some of the Charters of this date of the state of poverty and panic into which the monks had fallen. In the above Charter, which is by the half-roasted Abbot, Alan Stewart, in favour of James Stewart of Cardonald, a lease is given for five years of certain lands in the Regality of the Abbey, the lease including the "*Coal huich of Zellowlie*," now called Dalzellowlie. Another deed in favour of the same James Stewart mentions certain sums of money which he had expended on the repair of the Abbey, and assigns to him and his wife certain lands with teind sheaves, that is, the tenth sheaf taken from every harvest field; fishings and fisheries of the Water of Girvan, till it falls into the sea, with teinds of the fishing, etc.; also the forty shilling land of old extent of Craigoth (Craigoch), *with the Coalheuch of Zellowlie* within the said lands.

In 1569 another Charter was executed by the same Alan Stewart, this time in favour of the Laird of Brunstoun, William Kennedy, the Baillie of Carrick. He was the third husband of Black Bessy Kennedy of Brunstoune, sister to the Laird of Bargany. He had been lending a helping hand to the monks in their troubles. He had paid 1,000 merks for reparation of the Abbey, and had otherwise rendered them "help and assistance in this most perilous time in the necessaries of life." In return they transfer to him among other properties all and whole the six merk eight shilling and fourpenny land called Mains of Brunstoun, formerly called Nether Dalquharran, of old extent, with manor-place, fortalice, orchards, stallages or brewlands, *coal heuchs*, and *coal pots*, quarries, woods and groves, with the wood hag growing on said lands ; and in like manner the two mark land of Quarrelhill (elsewhere called Coralhill) and five shilling land of Glenord (Glenmard), etc. From the above items we can form a better conception of what Brunstone Castle and its surroundings were like 300 years ago. The coal field which now goes by the name of Kilgrammie was originally called Brunstone, and bore that name to comparatively modern times.

DRUMMOCHREEN COAL FIELD.

The minerals of Drummochreen are now and have long been in possession of Dalquharran. The surface belongs to Kilkerran. But in former times Drummochreen was a separate estate, and both the lands and the coal belonged to an old family, the Macalexanders, whose fair and spacious mansion adorned the north bank of the river a mile above the village. Only a bit of its wall remains to-day.

The first Macalexander of whom we have any record is described by the historian of the Kennedies as "ane proud man, but came to a bad end." Thomas Macalexander and several others "were ordainit to be tane to the Castel hill of Edinburgh, and there to be wirreit at ane stake "—in other words, to be hanged—"quhill they be dead, and all their lands, etc., to be forfaltit and escheit," for forging the King's coin. Sentence of forfeiture, however, was not carried out. This was in 1601. The next laird, John, did not take after his father, but devoted himself to legitimate industry. We find, from a contract of date 1617, undertaken by him, to supply twenty load of coals

to Kennedy of Bennane, that in his time—we do not know
how long before—coal was wrought on Drummochreen,
and that there was more than one pit going. That, however, does not mean anything very extensive, as the pits
were very shallow in those days, the coal being carried out
of the pits in creels, women being often employed as
carriers.

The next public record we have of the Drummochreen
coal industry is in the year 1701. In order to keep down
the water the colliers had erected a primitive hand pump,
which they were, or thought they were, under the necessity
of working on Sunday. The Kirk-Session heard of it, and
at their meeting on August 17th of that year appointed one
or more of their number to speak to the coal grieve "anent
his drawing water out of the hough of Dramochrein on
Sabbath day."

In the year 1726 the Session were again in difficulties in
regard to Sabbath profanation in the same neighbourhood.
This time the defaulters were Alexander Gordon, Wallace-
toun, and his whole family. Alexander wrote a letter to the
minister, which was read at a meeting on 15th December,
1726, acknowledging that he and his whole family were
guilty of working *through forgetfulness that it was the Sabbath
day*. This being a "singular case," the minister was asked
to take advice of some of his brethren of the Presbytery,
which he did, and the advice given and subsequently acted
on was that if the said family were penitent a sessional
rebuke and the same intimated from the pulpit would be
the most proper course. Accordingly Alexander, his wife,
family, and servants all appeared before the Session, and one

by one acknowledged their offence and their sorrow on account of it, and the following Sabbath, all the offenders, as enjoined by the Session, being present, the minister intimated the above acknowledgment to the congregation, whereupon, very much to the relief of all parties, the matter took end.

THE DALQUHARRAN PITS.*

When and where coal was first found on the estate I have no means of knowing. From various indications, it is probable that a commencement was made at a point near "the Colliers' Oak," a knotted and gnarled tree, evidently of great antiquity, which stands on the side of the road from Slatehouse to the Castle, and about 150 yards east of the Castle. The tree was so called because, according to tradition, the Laird of Dalquharran and the colliers were in the habit of meeting at that spot to discuss and settle matters of common interest.

Our forefathers would no sooner make a beginning than they would have to face the difficulty of getting rid of the water, which would accumulate all the more rapidly from the circumstance that the coal lies at an inclination. They were ingenious enough, however, to make the discovery that by driving a mine from the surface to the coal on a level or in such a way that the water would flow out by its own gravity, they would accomplish the two objects of getting rid of the water, and working the coal, as we say, "Level

---

* This article, inserted by the author as one of his series, was written by Mr. Francis Kennedy, and is now included to give completeness to the subject of this chapter.

free." A few yards east of the Colliers' Oak one of these "day levels," as they are called, was driven, which drained a portion of the coal near the outcrop.

Finding from experience the great advantage of getting coal level free, our ancestors set about cutting another day level. And they deserve credit for the way they have done it. Instead of cutting it from a low point in the coal measures, they now go to the lowest point they can find and begin it there. This point is about 100 yards west of Dowhail House, and only a few feet above the level of the river Girvan, and not many yards from the old channel.

The level itself bears traces of long and patient labour, which show the value put upon it in those early days. At the entrance it is protected by an arch, until a stratum of rock is reached strong enough to carry the surface. By this means, and with the assistance of one or two shafts in the vicinity of the Slatehouse—wrought, it is probable, by a windlass—perhaps one-fifth of the whole coal field was wrought level free.

We now come to the period of

INCLINES, OR INGAUN-EES (INGOING EYES).

One of these was made at the west end of Housemount House. Another, which was carried into the lower seams, started on the south side of the turnpike road in Wallace-town cowfield. While these and perhaps more places in the vicinity were being wrought in this way, the south end of Low Stables was where the horses used for drawing the coals out of the pits were stabled, and the north end the horsekeeper's house. Hence the name Old Stables, or Low

Stables, as it is now called. Other "ingoing eyes" were made further east at the Schoolhouse, the New Stables, and Craigieside Gardens.

THE GIN.

Going further east, a new chapter in the history of the coal workings is opened. We now find pits coming into use from which coals were drawn to the surface by a "gin." A gin consisted of a large wooden drum fixed to a shaft which was placed upright, the lower end turning on a pivot, the upper end being fixed to a cross beam by a journal. In this position the drum was at the upper end of the shaft, about 10 feet or 12 feet from the surface. Down near the surface a strong pole was fixed at a right angle from this shaft. A horse was attached to the end of the pole, and was driven round in a circle. As the horse was driven one way a creel of coals was raised to the surface on one side of the pit, while at the same time an empty creel was sent down on the other. The horse being now turned and driven the opposite way, more coals were brought up. This machine was used at a pit near Craigieside, and latterly in sinking the burning pit. There were other two pits further east than this gin pit. The one furthest east was in High Midton Garden. All the rise coal being wrought out, no more could be got out without driving to the dip of the day level. Accordingly, in 1827-28, a pit was put down at the Old Brick Work on the day level. This pit now goes under the name of

THE BURNING PIT.

This pit was 200 feet in depth, which implies that the

stoops around the pit supported a surface of that thickness. Further, the incline being 200 yards to the dip of the pit, and the inclination being at least one foot per yard, the stoops at the bottom of the incline must have supported a stratum of double the thickness or 400 feet. Notwithstanding this, the stoops at the bottom were made no larger than they were in the vicinity of the pit. Again, the parrot and corral coal stoops were placed *one above the other*, which would have been perfectly correct had the coal seams been flat, but they were not so. Consequently, to have had the under stoop in a position to have supported the upper, it should have been put as far to the dip of the upper as the difference between the perpendicular and the horizontal. From one or other of these causes, or both combined, in the year 1848—the year of much greater crashes above ground in the political world—about the middle of the last extension of the incline in the corral coal workings on the east side, the pillars commenced to break down. Men were employed to prop and build up the workings, but all their efforts were of no avail. The *creep* gradually extended away to the east and as far west as the whin dyke, which proved a barrier against it in this direction. From this point it gradually, day after day and week after week, travelled uphill, affecting all the seams in its course, until it became evident that a portion of the workings would entirely break down. A desperate effort was now made to save the incline by propping and building the workings on each side, but this had no effect in stopping the creep. At last, on 6th December, 1849, the whole workings from the eastern extremity to the whin dyke came down with one crash, shaking the whole surface as with the shock of an earthquake. Notwithstanding the serious aspect of matters previously, nobody about the place anticipated such a catastrophe. But the worst remains to be told. On that night, 6th December, or on the morning of 7th December, in consequence of the coal falling amongst the red-hot bricks of the engine furnace, the workings took fire. At five o'clock in the morning the fire was so strong that the flames reached the top of the pit, a distance of 200 feet, and set the pithead frame in a blaze.

All the attempts to extinguish the fire were unsuccessful, and it continued to make rapid progress. It appeared to come direct from the pit to the surface, and also to spread along west to the whin dyke above Wallacetown and east to another whin dyke beyond Craigieside. The whole brow of the hill between these two points was red-hot for many years. These two dykes, however, proved to be effectual barriers to the spread of the fire east and west. After all the coals near the outcrop were burned, the fire gradually crept away down the workings, and the surface became cooler, until, at the present day, the main evidence that the fire still exists is the constant discharge of gases from the cracks and rents on the surface.

DALZELLOWLIE PIT FIRE.

The history of mining in the valley of the Girvan has been very chequered. In the year 1835 the "sitting" of the Kilgrammie pit took place, and the imprisonment of John

Brown in a living grave for twenty-three days. A few years later there occurred the "sit" in the Dalquharran workings and the subsequent fire which is still smouldering. At a more remote period the other pit higher up the water, Dalzellowlie, now discontinued, also had its share in misfortune. At the middle of the last century it took fire, and after burning for about one hundred years, at last burned itself out. At the period when the fire broke out, the coal field belonged partly to Kilkerran and partly to Culzean. Coal was dug here as far back as the 15th century. When we picture to ourselves the coal-mining of these primitive times, we must dissociate our mind from steam engines, and, indeed, machinery of all kinds, even the "gin," and think of the miners, including women and children, tramping down from the surface into black caverns with wicker baskets, *creels*, on their backs, and then when they were filled toiling and staggering back with them to the surface. At that early period the land and the coal field under it were part of the rich revenues of the Abbey of Crossraguel. In the old charters of the Abbey the name is given as "Yellowlie." Whether before the Reformation, or in the course of the general scramble for the Church lands and property which followed the Reformation, we do not know, but the coal field came to be jointly possessed by Kilkerran and Culzean. There were frequent disputes between the two proprietors as to their rights, and at one time these disputes took shape in a "gude gangin' law plea," of which a bulky record is or used to be in the library of Kilkerran.

The pit took fire in the year 1749. Our authority is the Rev.

Matthew Biggar of Kirkoswald, within whose parish the pit was situated, though the district is now within the new Parish of Crosshill. Mr. Biggar wrote a description of his parish for Sir John Sinclair's "Statistical Account of Scotland." The volume of the statistical account in which his article appears was published in 1794. He says:—"The coal mine of Dalzellowlie set on fire 45 years ago and is still burning. Several methods have been tried to extinguish the fire, but they have proved ineffectual. It has been the opinion of the best coal miners in the West of Scotland that, if no part of the coal near the fire were to be wrought for a number of years, it would of course soon be extinguished. This method has accordingly been adopted, and the fire has gradually lessened. The want of coal has been a great loss to the parish, as it was a valuable mine consisting of five seams of coal from six to fifteen feet thick."

How the pit took fire is not upon record. There would be easy access to it from the surface through one of the "ingaun-ees." There is a tradition that two herd laddies for a boyish freak one day crept down into the darkness and kindled a fire with sticks, the result being that the coal took fire. Another traditional version is that either the Culzean men or the Kilkerran men had long been working over the march, and to cover their delinquency and save themselves and their masters from the consequences, had wilfully fired the pit. Being wrought from the surface and with the cracking of the ground as the fire increased, it was found to be impossible to exclude the air; and it continued to burn until within the memory of people—though there must be few—still living. Part of the coal could still be wrought, although in the neighbourhood of the fire the heat was so great that the men had to work stripped to the trousers. The warmth on the surface told in the rapid growth of the young wood planted on the hill, and there was not a part of Kilkerran woods that brought in a better return.

There was another way in which the misfortune became an advantage, though it was a more questionable one. Illegal distillation used to be carried on in our valley. There was a famous still on the banks of the Lady Glen, and there are traces of others elsewhere. A great trouble with the smugglers was the getting rid of the smoke from the still with the least risk of detection. Sometimes it was carried along the surface for a considerable distance in trenches covered over with stones and turf to some outlet where what remained of the smoke might be safely left to find its way to the upper air. There are traces of such trenches on the banks of the Penquhapple ravine at Knockgerran, and at Littleton, where the burn flowing through Trolorg farm enters the Penquhapple, and there is a small cave with the remains of a well. It is said that the smugglers in the upper end of the valley fell upon a still more simple and ingenious method of escaping detection by carrying on their operations in the Dalzellowlie pit, and that latterly the smoke which was seen oozing to the surface at the "reekin' stane" had another source than the burning of the coal field. The same clever rogues found another wall of defence in the superstition of the district. One of them occasionally dressed up for the part of a ghost so that the neighbourhood got the reputation of being haunted, and the inhabitants gave the burning hills by night as wide a berth as possible. There may be people still living—at all events there were not many years ago—who, as young men, knew the flavour of the brew in the burning pit.

CHAPTER X.

NOTABLE MEN.

HEW AINSLIE.

HEW AINSLIE first saw the light at Butler's Brae, Bargany,
on 5th April, 1792. Across the river from Bargany House,
rising from the level along which runs the carriage drive, is
a sloping and wooded bank. That is the Butler's Brae,
and at the foot, about a hundred yards from the bridge,
stood the cottage where the poet was born. There are no
traces of it now. The father, George Ainslie, was baker to
Bargany, and he named his son after the laird, Sir Hew
Dalrymple Hamilton. Hew being delicate from his birth,
his father got a tutor to teach him at home. Afterwards
he was sent to the Parish School of Ballantrae, and finally
to the Ayr Academy. He returned home at the age
of 14. At this time Sir Hew was engaged in an
extension plan for the improvement of the estate, under
the direction of the celebrated landscape gardener, White,
by whom a number of young men, mostly from the South,
were employed. Young Ainslie joined them, as he says,
"to harden my constitution, and check my overgrowth."
The young men got up a private theatre in a granary,

130

performing "The Gentle Shepherd," "Douglas," &c., young Ainslie acting the part of Jenny in the former, and thus acquiring his first relish for sentimental song. Afterwards his father removed to Roslin, and in his 17th year Hew was sent to Glasgow to study law, but did not take kindly to it. Soon after he got a situation in the Register House, Edinburgh, which he retained till 1822, being part of the time amanuensis to the famous philosopher, Professor Dugald Stewart. He married in 1812, when he was only 20. Children came in due course, and his salary being quite inadequate to the demands upon it, he resolved to emigrate. Landing in New York in July, 1822, he purchased a small farm in the State of New York, and resided there for three years. He then made a trial of Robert Owen's settlement in Indiana, but, finding it a failure, he removed to Cincinnati, where he entered into partnership with a firm of brewers. In 1829 he established a branch of the business at Louisville, which, three years later, was ruined by an inundation of the Ohio. His usual ill fortune followed him in another establishment of the same kind which he had started in Indiana, and which was destroyed by fire in 1834. Latterly, and till his retirement from active life, he was employed in superintending the erection of mills, factories, and breweries in the United States.

In 1864 he visited Scotland and received a warm welcome, the literary men of Glasgow and Edinburgh showing him flattering marks of attention. He died at Louisville, U.S., on 11th March, 1878, aged 86.

Ainslie was a poet from his early years. A visit which

he paid to Ayrshire, after his removal to Edinburgh, led to his writing " A Pilgrimage to the Land of Burns," in which, amid descriptions in prose of no great literary value, he incorporated most of his songs. From the want of an influential publisher the work fell almost still-born from the press. In 1855, at New York, he published "Scottish Songs, Ballads and Poems." Many of his compositions are to be found in *Whistle Binkie, Gems of Scottish Song,* and other collections.

If Ainslie's lyre is deficient in some of the higher and more spiritual chords, yet, for natural pathos, for sympathy with Nature's varying moods, for broad humour, for strong patriotism, and not least for his command of genuine Scottish Doric, he is well entitled to the high place which he continues to hold among Scottish poets of the second rank. Dailly may well be proud of him.

One of his most famous pieces is the following :

DOWIE IN THE HINT O' HAIRST.

It's dowie in the hint o' hairst,
   At the wa'-gang o' the swallow,
When the wind grows cauld, and the burns grow bauld,
   And the wuds are hanging yellow ;
But oh, its dowier far to see
   The wa'-gang o' her the heart gangs wi',
The dead-set o' a shinin' e'e,
   That darkens the wearie warld on thee.

There was mickle love atween us twa—
   Oh ! twa could ne'er be fonder—
And the thing on yerd was never made
   That could hae gart us sunder.
But the way o' Heaven's abune a' ken—
   An' we maun bear what it likes to sen'—

It's comfort, though, to wearie men,
    That the warst o' this warld's waes maun end.

There's mony things that come an' gae—
    Just kent and just forgotten—
And the flowers that busk a bonnie brae
    Gin anither year lie rotten.
But the last look o' that lovely e'e,
    And the dying grip she ga'e to me,
They're settled like eternitie—
    Oh ! Mary, that I were wi' thee !

HAMILTON PAUL.

In the early days of the coal industry the custom prevailed, of which Dalquharran is now almost the only survival in Scotland, of the proprietors of the land retaining the working of the coal in their own hands, a manager or grieve, paid by and responsible to the estate, being employed. Till near the end of the 18th century the Bargany coal field was wrought on the north bank of the Girvan opposite Bargany House. It might seem strange that the laird should have had a going colliery almost within a stone-cast of his front door, and in full view of his windows. But we must bear in mind that before the days of steam and when the coal was brought to the surface by the slow process of winding, by means of a horse or "gin," a colliery would not be so much of a blot on the landscape as it is now. For many years the situation of Bargany coal grieve was held by a man of the name of John Paul. John was a rough and passionate man. At the same time he was shrewd and pawky. At one time the Ballantrae people got the idea into their heads that there might be coal along their shore, and sent for John to examine and report. John knew "what was what, fu' brawly," but to please them he went, and after kneeling down on the shore and smelling the ground round about him, rose and said, with a solemn shake of the head, "Boys, there's nae coal here."

In the year 1773 we find John occupying the same cottage at Butler's Brae which, a few years later, came to be the residence of George Ainslie, the Bargany baker, the change of occupancy being probably owing to the opening of a pit or pits at Kilgrammie or the neighbourhood, which rendered it necessary that John should take up his quarters there. In the above year there was a son born to him at Butler's Brae, whom he named after the laird, Hamilton.

Besides Hamilton, he had other two sons, and all three showed signs of a rhyming gift, judging from stories of *impromptu* verse-making sometimes indulged in by the boys around the fireside. Hamilton received his early education in the parish school, where, at this time, not only Latin but French was taught. He seems to have gone straight from the parish school to Glasgow University, which he entered to study for the Church. There he had for his class-mate a Glasgow lad named Thomas Campbell, who afterwards became the world-famous poet. An intimacy soon sprang up between the two kindred spirits. In a competition, which both entered, for the best poem on a given subject, Hamilton carried off the prize. For some time during his student career he was tutor to a family in Argyllshire, and as Campbell held a similar appointment in the same county, their intimacy was kept up, and a correspondence, mostly poetical, was carried on between them. On getting license Hamilton returned to Ayrshire, and had to continue as a probationer for 13 years, during which he acted as assistant to several ministers. He also wrote for, and for a time, we believe, edited, the *Ayr Advertiser*. At length, at the age of 40, he got a presentation to the picturesque Parish of Broughton, where he spent the remainder of his days.

In 1819 he published an edition of Burns, with a memoir, which received high commendation from Professor Wilson (Christopher North). In the following year he published "a few specimens preparatory to a larger collection which he had in contemplation," and which he entitled "A foretaste of pleasant things," but he never appears to have carried out his larger design. Most of his poems were only published in the newspapers and periodicals of the day, and very many of them have been lost. He composed with rapidity and ease, and many of his effusions were dashed off at a sitting.

As showing the estimation in which he was held as a poet by some of his contemporaries, we quote from Hew Ainslie, who says that when the Burns Club was founded at Alloway, Paul furnished an annual ode, and when Chalmers, who was then engaged in his great work, "Caledonia," read one of them in the Ayr newspaper, he wrote from London to a friend that he would give all Ayrshire for copies of the previous eight odes.

One of the best things he ever did was to save the Auld Brig o' Doon. Indeed, he may be said to have saved it twice over. At the time when he was resident in Ayr as a probationer, the Road Trustees had contracted for the building of the new bridge, and had actually sold the old one to the contractor as a quarry. No sooner was he informed of this intended act of sacrilege than Paul at once wrote the "Petition of the Auld Brig o' Doon," which was printed and circulated over the country, and in two or three days a sufficient sum was subscribed to re-purchase the materials of the old bridge, and also to keep it in repair. A good many years afterwards the waters of the Doon had so much undermined the buttresses of the old bridge that it seemed to be in danger of coming down. David Auld, an Ayr barber or hairdresser, who had made a fortune by the exhibition of Thom's statues of Tam o' Shanter and Souter Johnny, and who built the inn and shell palace in the neighbourhood of Burns's Monument, applied to the Trustees for money to prevent the ruin of the old fabric, but he was told that as it was only a private footpath, the Trustees would not be justified in applying any portion of their funds for such a purpose. Thereupon Mr. Auld sent them copies of the poetical petition which had formerly saved the bridge, and of which the Trustees were ignorant. On reading it they at once contributed privately the sum that was necessary to complete the required repairs.

When he became too infirm for the duties of his charge, an assistant was appointed, who was so popular that people came from the country round about to hear him. "So," said the old minister grimly, "you think yourself a very big man because you are followed by the multitudes. Let me tell you, my man, a still greater crowd would gather to see you hanged."

Though always a great favourite in female society, he never married. He died at Broughton Manse, in February, 1854, aged 81.

The following is

THE PETITION OF THE AULD BRIG O' DOON.

Must I, like modern fabrics of a day,
Decline, unwept, the victim of decay?
Shall my bold arch, which proudly stretches o'er
Doon's classic stream from Kyle to Carrick shore,
Be suffered in oblivion's gulf to fall,
And hurl to wreck my venerable wall?
Forbid it every tutelary power
That guards my keystone at the midnight hour;
Forbid it ye, who, charmed by Burns's lay,
Amid those scenes can linger out the day.
Let Nanny's sark and Maggie's mangled tail
Plead in my cause and in the cause prevail,
The man of taste who comes my form to see
And curious asks, but asks in vain for me,
With tears of sorrow will my fate deplore,
When he is told " the Auld Brig is no more."
Stop then; oh, stop the more than vandal rage
That marks this revolutionary age,
And bid the structure of your fathers last,
The pride of this, the boast of ages past;
For never let your children's children tell,
By your decree the fine old fabric fell.

THOMAS THOMSON—A FRIEND OF SIR WALTER SCOTT.

Thomas Thomson, who is described by competent judges as "the most learned and exact investigator of his time," was born in the Manse of Dailly in 1768. Not only his father, but his grandfather and grand-uncle were ministers of the Church of Scotland, the former in Auchtermuchty, the latter in Elgin. Thomas received his early education at the Parish School, and at the age of 14 entered the University of Glasgow, where he took his degree in 1789. It had been the wish of his father, rather than his own, that he should study for the Church, but an event now occurred by which his thoughts and career were turned in another direction, and that was the acquaintance which he formed through Lord Kilkerran with Lord Hailes, son-in-law to Kilkerran, and the first of Scottish critical enquirers. In 1793 we find him established in Edinburgh studying law and living in lodgings in Bristo Street along with his younger brothers.

It was at this time that Thomas formed a friendship with Sir Walter Scott, which continued till the death of the latter in 1832. Scott became a frequent visitor at Bristo Street. He got into the way of dropping in at breakfast-time on Sunday mornings, and John used to speak with delight of the conversations between Scott and his brother at these meetings. Sir Walter is said to have been indebted to Mr. Thomson for some of his materials. There can be no doubt he would draw from such a mine of Scottish historical research for historical materials. It is supposed that some of his names were taken from this district, and were suggested to him by his friend. No doubt Scott was in the habit of coining, and showed great genius in coining significant names, and it may be thought that some of the following were so coined. But he sometimes found such names ready made, and it seems not unlikely that hearing some of our names from his friend, his quick instinct at once appropriated them. For example, " Lady Glowre-owrum," which may be taken from our Glowreowrum, abbreviated Glowrie, so called from the wide prospect over the lower portion of our valley. "Habakkuk Mucklewrath," the name of the half-insane covenanting preacher in "Old Mortality," may be from M'Ilwraith, anciently spelt M'Lewrath, a common name in former times, as it still is, in the district. "Dreepdaily" may have been suggested by the name of the parish, as well as by the rainy character of our western climate. Again Scott's "Cleikumin" may have been taken from the house of that name which stood on the old Bargany Road, near Lady Farm. But this is more doubtful, as there are several Cleikumins in the country.

With all his vast knowledge of constitutional and legal antiquities he never could be prevailed upon to commit himself to authorship, partly from modesty, but in part also from procrastination, which was one of his weaknesses, and of which he gave an example in the epitaph for the famous philosopher, Dugald Stewart, which he was asked to write. He began it, but it was never finished. A great deal of his learned investigations has thus been lost.

He had a tall, erect figure. His features were plain, but not commonplace, and expressive of benevolence. He was marked by entire freedom from affectation, and a manly simplicity of manner and language. His portrait is in the National Portrait Gallery in Edinburgh.

He died at Shrubhill, near Dryburgh, in 1852, at the age of 84.

JOHN THOMSON OF DUDDINGSTON.

The most famous of the men of our parish is the Rev.

John Thomson, one of the greatest of Scottish artists—
certainly the greatest Scottish landscape painter of his
time, styled "The Scottish Claude Lorraine," commonly
known as Thomson of Duddingston. He was the fourth
and youngest son of the Rev. Thomas Thomson, who was
minister of this parish for nearly 43 years. He was born
in the Manse of Dailly on 1st September, 1778. He was
destined by his father for the ministry, but his tastes lay in
a different direction. Even at an early age, art, his future
mistress, had claimed him as her own. When his father
intimated to him his wish that he should be a minister, he
went down on his knees before him, and, with tears in his
eyes, implored him to make him a painter. The old
gentleman merely patted him on the head and bade him go
to his book and learn his lessons. From early boyhood he
was more of a student of Nature than of books, delighting
to roam among the beautiful surroundings of the Manse,
frequently rising at two o'clock on a summer morning to
see the rising sun from the top of Hadyet or Kirkhill, or
to witness the peculiar effect of its rays penetrating the
trees in a neighbouring wood. Even in boyhood his pencil
was prolific. But he was quite independent both of pencil
and paper, as could be seen on the walls of the Manse,
both inside and out, which contained many of his sketches,
executed with the ends of burnt sticks, the snuffings of
candles, or anything else he could procure that would do.
His father, while amused at his precocity, still held by his
purpose that he should study for the Church.

In addition to the ordinary studies for the ministry,
young Thomson devoted himself to physical science, such

as it was in those days, inheriting his father's tastes in this direction, and became proficient in astronomy, geology, optics, and chemistry.

At the early age of 21 he was licensed to preach the Gospel by the Presbytery of Ayr, and there seems to have been no difficulty about his being presented by the Crown, the patron, in succession to his father, which took place in the year 1800. Not long after he was settled he married Miss Ramsay, daughter of the minister of Kirkmichael. He still continued to pursue his favourite studies. He was frequently to be seen in the woods of Bargany with his sketchbook or easel. An old man, still alive [1883], remembers seeing him sitting for hours before an old tree at Old Maxwelton. Meantime his reputation was growing, but not in his own parish. The Dailly people did not like such exclusive devotion to art, to the neglect, as they thought, of his proper work. There were stories about the Sabbath day being partly given up to art at the Manse. And there were some of his pictures, caricatures, so droll that some of the douce parishioners shook their heads over them. At the same time there were some of the Sabbath critics who began to think that the minister's preaching was not quite orthodox. A few left the church and travelled all the way to the Burgher meeting-house at Maybole, and altogether there was so much dissatisfaction in the parish that the Presbytery felt called upon to interfere, and appointed one of their older members to have a private interview with Mr. Thomson, and remonstrate with him on the subject of these grievances. Mr. Thomson listened to his rebuker in silence, and appeared to be greatly affected by them—with downward eyes fixed on his nervous fingers, giving only an occasional modest glance at the face of his rebuker. The old man was pleased, thinking he had made a good impression, and resolved that he would make a favourable report to the Presbytery. Little did he know that all the time young Thomson was sketching, or rather etching, a laughable likeness of his rebuker with a pin upon his thumb-nail.

It is not to be wondered at that Mr. Thomson should have desired a change. Accordingly when Duddingston, a beautiful parish in the neighbourhood of Edinburgh, behind Arthur's Seat, became vacant, he and his friends took steps which were successful to secure the appointment. Here his talents found more scope and encouragement. His fame as a landscape painter continued to spread. He was early admitted an honorary member of the Royal Scottish Academy, and his works continued year after year to grace the walls of its exhibitions. His Dailly pictures were for the most part gifted away to friends. But he was now induced to put a money value on his talents. For the first picture he sold he was offered 15 guineas. He himself thought this was too much, and it was only when a friend, in whose judgment he had confidence, told him it was worth three times the money, that he could be persuaded to accept. Commissions for pictures poured in upon him from all parts, till his profits reached the sum of about £1,800 a year. The Manse was famed for hospitality. Walter Scott, John Clerk of Eldin, afterwards Lord Eldin, Sir T. Dick Lauder, and most of the leading counsel at the Scottish Bar were frequent visitors, and few strangers of distinction in art came to Edinburgh without calling on Thomson of Duddingston. Meantime it is said that he did not neglect his ministerial duties, and that he found time for indulging his tastes in other directions. He had attained considerable proficiency in music, and could play with ease on the violin and flute. At the same time he kept pace with the science and thought of the day, and when his brother Thomas, along with other eminent Edinburgh literateurs, had succeeded in starting the *Edinburgh Review*, John wrote several articles for some of its earlier numbers on the subject of physical science which were greatly admired at the time for their clear and vigorous style.

Towards the beginning of 1840 Mr. Thomson's health began to decline, and during the summer and autumn he grew worse. By the middle of October he was confined to a sickbed. On the 26th an old pupil arrived on a visit. Mr. Thomson felt weaker than usual, and had a strong presentiment that that was the last day he had to live. The day had been bright and beautiful, and the sun was setting in glory. He requested his friend to help his son to wheel the bed towards the window that he might behold the scene, on which he had so often feasted his eyes, for the last time. He continued to gaze till he fainted from weakness. This was his last effort. Falling into a quiet slumber, he passed away the following day—another sunset after a day of brightness. He died in his 62nd year. It is unnecessary to particularise, even if we could, Mr.

Thomson's pictures. Landscape was his forte. He was fond of depicting ancient castles and decayed fortresses, such as Queen Mary's Castle of Craigmillar, of which he has given various views, and other ruins along the east coast. In the West he had many subjects from the Trossachs, Loch Lomond, Loch Etive, Dunstaff- nage Castle, Dunluce, Wolf's Crag, &c. One of his happiest efforts was a small picture of Loch Achray. There may be others of his pictures, the subjects of which lie in our parish, in existence, but the only one, so far as we are aware, is the old Castle of Kilkerran, which hangs in the dining-room of Kilkerran House.

APPENDIX I.

DAILLY PLACE-NAMES.

Auchneight, Mid Auchneight, Easter Auchneight—
Within the grounds of Bargany.

Balceachy—Probably another form of Balcletchie.

Balcroy—On Knockgerran, about 100 yards west of the
road end.

Baldrynan—About a quarter of a mile east of High
Newlands.

Barclonoquhan—A mansion-house or castle on or near
the site of the present House of Kilkerran.

Berry Knoll or Berry Knowes—Above Lovestone
Hill, about 10 yards west of the stone quarry.

Black Park—In the wood to the north of Romilly Pit.

Blaweary—On the Farm of Lochrie.

Boghead—On the west side of the road above Heather
Row.

Burnfoot—At the junction of the Dobbingston and
Lindsayston Burns.

Camlachie—Opposite Penkill Castle, on the south side of
Penquhapple Burn.

CARSKULL—Below Glenwells on Drummochreen Farm.

CAULD SPRINGS—On Glenton Farm, on the south side of the old Maybole Road.

CLACHANEASY SPOUT—Near Camregan, on the south side of the road between the trough and Camregan.

CLACHANPLUCK—Near Kilkerran House.

CLAYCROFT—Between Plantainhead and the road to Blair

CORALHILL—Also Quarrelhill and Quarryhill.

CORSERUNNEL—In the neighbourhood of Roughneuk.

CRAIGENQUARRY—On Moorston Farm.

CRAIGENSOLUS—Between Lane and Maxwelton.

CURRACHAN — Above Woodend on Moorston side of Filfarquhar Burn.

DAILY KEG—Near Romilly Pit.

DALQUHIR—On the right bank of the Penquhapple Burn, near where it enters the river.

DALREACHIE—In the Toddy Glen above Kilkerran House.

DIRTY DUBS—Near Drummochreen Farmhouse at the side of the burn.

DRONGAN—On Drongan Burn, on the upper side of the carriage drive to Kilkerran.

DRONGAN—On the old road to Girvan in Maxwelton Holm.

ELDINTON—On Maxwelton Farm to the east of Dailly water reservoir, where John Semple the Covenanter was shot.

ENTRYHEAD OF DRUMMOCHREEN—The old house by the river.

FALTRIPLOCH—At the lower end of the present curling pond.

FARDENCHRAICHER—Opposite Laigh Threave.

FILFARQUHAR—At the bend of the road to Poundland.

GALLOWHILL—On the knoll on the north side of the avenue to Bargany House, about 100 yards from S.W. Gatehouse.

GARRYHORN—Near Glengie, where there used to be free-stone quarry.

GATESIDE OF DRUMELLAN—Between Pathhead and the road.

GIGMAGOG.—The name, which is sometimes given to Mains Cottages, was originally applied to a large boulder which lay between the cottage and the river. It was broken up and taken for the erection of the monument to Sir Charles Fergusson on Kildoon Hill.

GLENGIE—On the road leading from above Poundland to Kilkerran House, on the Glengie Burn.

GLENMARD—Behind Kilgrammie House.

GLENSIDE OF MERKLAND — On the west side of the Filfarquhar Glen, about 100 yards from the Maybole Road, on Moorston Farm.

HOLEHOUSE, HOLE OF LANE, OR LOCKSTOWN IN HOLE OF LANE—On the Knockgerran side of the burn which constitutes the march between Knockgerran and Glengennet.

JUNIPER KNOWES—At the head of the Weavers' Glen, Bargany.

KNOCKAVISH—Below Lochmoddy Toll on the west side of Lochmoddy Burn.

KNOCKCRINDLE—To the west of the Heather Row.

KORALSCRAFT—On the top of Meg's Hill.

LADYWELL, OR MY LADY'S WELL—Near Glengie.

LANNILANE—The house at the old lime work on Blair Hill.

MACHRYKILL—The site of the old Celtic Chapel on White-hill Farm.

MAVIS NEST—On the burn at the back of Galanston.

MIDTON OF CAMREGAN—Between Old Dailly and Cam-regan on the south side of the road, where John Stevenson the Covenanter lived.

MILCAVISH—The name originally given to the village of New Dailly. The name occurs in 1720.

MULLOCKSTON — Probably what is now called High Mullocks.

MUIRYETT OR MOORGATE—Where Low Craighead Farm-steading now stands.

MUTTONHALL—On Camregan, about a quarter of a mile up the old wood road running up the hill from near the drinking trough.

PENBLEATH — Also Easter and Wester Penbleath on Dobbingston Farm.

PETHMOUTH—In the Weavers' Glen, Bargany.

PROMISE PUMP—On the Maitland approach to Kilkerran House, corrupted from "Primrose," the name of the man who used to be employed to carry water to the house.

ROYAL OAK—On the old road at the Bargany pond.

SCARHEAD—Opposite Lindsayston, on the Balcamey side of the burn.

SHAKSISTON, SHAKISTON, SHAKSHAWSTON, or SHAWSTON—Near Drumgirvan Bridge, on the upper side of the present carriage drive to Kilkerran.

SILLYHOLE—Near the foot of the " Bellman's Brae," that is, the brae between the Barr Road and Woodend. The church-officer, or bellman, lived here, hence the name.

STRANIGOWER—On the south side of the " Minister's Brae," between Goudieholm and Moorston March.

STYEHOWIE—In Penquhapple Glen.

TEN SHILLING LAND — Between the Romilly Pit and Slatehouse.

WATSHOUSE—Also called Watchhouse, was on the Bargany road, near the village.

WAUKMILL OF DRUMMOCHREEN—On the river near the Old House, where, as we find from Abercrummie's account, there was a waukmill as well as a cornmill 200 years ago.

WHITESTANECRAFT—A little to the N.W. of Romilly Pit.

WOODNEUK—Behind Woodend.

APPENDIX II.

LIST OF MINISTERS OF DAILLY PARISH SINCE 1574.

THE records commence in 1574, two years after the death of John Knox.

JOHN CUNNINGHAM, 1574-1589.

DAVID BARCLAY, 1590-1599.

JAMES INGLIS, 1605-1640.

JOHN INGLIS, 1641-1659.
> (Brother of the preceding.)

ANDREW MILLAR, A.M., 1660-1666 (?).
> (An " outed " minister.)

THOMAS SKINNER, A.M., 1666-1688 (?).
> (Rabbled at the Revolution.)

PATRICK CRAWFORD, A.M., 1691-1710.

WILLIAM STEEL, 1711-1723.

WILLIAM PATOUN, 1724-1755.

THOMAS THOMSON, 1756-1799.

JOHN THOMSON, 1800-1805.
> (The famous artist : *See* chap. x.)

CHARLES CUNNINGHAM, 1806-1815.

ALEXANDER HILL, D.D., 1816-1840.
> (Became Professor of Divinity in Glasgow University and Moderator of the General Assembly.)

WILLIAM CHALMERS, D.D., 1841-1843.
>   (Joined the Free Church at the Disruption
>   and afterwards became Principal of the
>   English Presbyterian Church College in
>   London.)

DAVID STRONG, 1843-1855.
CORNELIUS GIFFEN, D.D., 1855-1869.
GEORGE TURNBULL, D.D., 1869-1908.

www.ingramcontent.com/pod-product-compliance
Lightning Source LLC
Chambersburg PA
CBHW060402030726

47497CB00003B/827